MARIE-HÉLÈNE LEBEAULT

AUTHOR OF THE EVERS SERIES

THE QUEST

FOR THE

CURSED

MIRRORS

DEFENDERS OF THE REALM - BOOK FIVE

BEACHES AND TRAILS
PUBLISHING

ABOUT THE AUTHOR

Marie-Helene Lebeault lives in Quebec, Canada and is the mother of two young adults. A retired teacher, she now spends her days writing, translating academic manuals, and lending her voice to corporate training videos. She enjoys reading, hiking, and going to the beach. She is also an avid rollercoaster fiend and is on a mission to visit all the Six Flags amusement parks with her daughter. Every year, she travels for three weeks on a solo adventure to a new part of the world.

Follow on Social Media, she'd love to hear from you!

Website Email Newsletter

facebook.com/mhlebeaultauthor

x.com/mhlebeault

instagram.com/mhlebeault

amazon.com/author/mhlebeault

bookbub.com/authors/marie-helene-lebeault

goodreads.com/mhlebeault

linkedin.com/in/mhlebeault

tiktok.com/@mhlebeaultauthor

youtube.com/@mhlebeault

ALSO BY THE AUTHOR

The Chronicles of the Starborne Cadets

Stars Beyond Realms

Shadows of Orion

Echoes of the Void

The Nebula's Heart

The Starborne Paradox

Defenders of the Realm

A Journey to Power

The Quest for the Emerald Rattleback

A Summer of Discovery

The Quest for the Sacred Tree

A Summer of Opposites

The Quest for the Phantom Feather

A Summer of Courage

The Quest for the Kraken's Ink

A Summer of Destiny

The Quest for the Cursed Mirrors

The Evers Series

The Ancestors' Key

The Academy

The Time Walker

The World Jumper

Blood Magick Trilogy

The Blood Mage

Blood Magick

Blood Legacy

Standalones

Clarity Castle

What Happens Next?

Ghost Stories

Holiday Shifters

Echoes of Tomorrow

Utopia

Picture Books

Fairy Grandmother: Millie Goes to Antarctica

Fairy Grandmother: Millie Goes to the North Pole

Fairy Grandmother: Millie Goes to China

Fairy Grandmother: Millie Goes to Africa

(Also available in French, Spanish, German, and Italian)

CHAPTER
ONE

Herja sat in one of the overstuffed chairs, looking over the Institute grounds, a strange melancholy washing over her. It was the first day of classes... and the last first day she would have here as a student. She and all her friends were eighteen and in their fifth, final year at the Institute.

Herja didn't do all that good with change, and even though she'd had five years to prepare for this moment, it seemed to have stuck up on her like a cat stalking a rodent. She had her plans for what would happen after graduation, of course.

But... it somehow didn't seem like enough.

Her mate, Wickham, sat on the edge of her chair. He'd always been lean and lanky, but over the summer, he'd stuck to an impressive workout schedule and had bulked up. His muscles were still lean but more pronounced now.

"You doing all right?" he asked, a concerned frown on his face. "Penelope told us that Odele got you pretty good in sparring today."

Herja shook herself, freeing herself from these melancholy thoughts. "Oh, I'm fine. I was just getting caught up in my head. How was your day?"

"Good." Wickham stood and pulled another chair over to sit on.

Their other friends were entering the fifth-year dorm now, and Herja waved them over. Wickham continued as they all got settled.

"Professor Carmilla is more strict than West and Ealdwulf were last year," he said. "She insists that since this is our last year, we need to be very serious. We spent the whole day discussing our spell books and how important they were."

Here, Kaia made a face. She and Wickham shared the silver hair that all witches had, and she folded her arms over her plump chest. "I tried to ask when we'd actually be putting them together and she wouldn't say."

"She does seem to have a strict idea of how this year should go," Raven agreed.

They wore a powder blue face veil that covered their eyes today— the same color as Penelope's uniform. Raven was a gorgon rather than a witch, but the kingdom of Eldavon hadn't had gorgons for centuries —they didn't know how to train Raven, and so Raven was paired with the witches since their magic seemed to be more of the spell sort, rather than the innate type that dragons had.

Speaking of—

"How did the first day go with you two?" Kaia asked, looking between Penelope and Herja. "Nolen told me that Odele and Herja got a little too real with sparring."

"We were given a very serious talk about the importance of this year's training," Penelope sighed. "How normally we'd be training in elements about evacuating people or fighting natural disasters. But we're learning actual military techniques instead. Professor Under-wood was very grim about it all."

Herja nodded, her own expression grim. "It seems like Eldavon is preparing for the possibility of war."

The mood turned somber at her words.

"We will not have a war," Wickham said. Tension laced his voice, even though he tried to force it to be upbeat. "We thought we might end up fighting with Odentia, and look at how that has resolved itself."

Herja shook her head. She understood the desire not to think about that frightening possibility, but it was still hanging over them. "Not with Odentia, though. A bunch of the other kingdoms are suffering from droughts and severe losses because of natural disasters. A few are accepting help from Eldavon, but others..."

She sighed heavily as she shook her head again. Once, she would have thought she could solve it all, but now she knew these things weren't so easily fixed.

Kaia tightened her arms. "It's not just them that are suffering. Eldavon doesn't have a lot to give, either."

Herja turned to her, her stomach twisting.

"Should we really be talking about this?" Penelope asked bleakly. "I mean, we won't change anything, and all we're going to do is increase our own anxiety."

"I want to know what's happening," Herja insisted.

Raven took Penelope's hand. "It is good to be prepared. My dreams have been filled with dry fields and dying crops. Why doesn't Eldavon have a lot to give, Kaia?"

"You know my parents are in agriculture," she started.

Wickham shifted in his seat. "I thought your dad retired."

"He went back since I'm eighteen now, and he was needed," Kaia explained. "Anyway. The winter was so hot and dry that our water tables were low all across the kingdom. Lots of streams and rivers are drying up because there wasn't enough melt to keep them going."

Herja thought about how she had enjoyed lazing about in the sun all winter and her stomach twisted further.

"And summer didn't help," Penelope murmured. "There were a record number of fires."

Kaia nodded. "Summer baked the land, and we have little to harvest. The Crown has been distributing food from the stores. We have enough to keep Eldavon going for about seven years of drought, but not if we're going to share. And if we have food when the other kingdoms don't..."

She trailed off, wincing.

Herja ran her fingers through her short black hair. That was grim news. She didn't like the idea of anyone starving. If they only had a limited amount of food, would they have to pick and choose who ate and who did not?

"Hopefully, it'll be a better winter," she said aloud.

"The weather patterns that started last year are continuing now," Kaia said, sounding somewhat reluctant. "My parents think this winter will be just as dry as last year."

Penelope nodded, looking worried as she brushed her fire-red hair off her shoulders. "The Fire Watch is still fighting a bunch of the fires that erupted last year. They're working hard to recruit new people because we're exhausted."

Wickham groaned as he leaned back. "This isn't what I wanted to think about today."

Herja winced as she reached over for Wickham's hand. "Sorry. But in good news, Odentia and Eldavon's relationship has never been stronger. It seems Queen Rowena is much more reasonable than her father."

To her surprise, Wickham's expression only darkened. He scowled as he shook his head. "Yeah, I've heard about that, too. She's going to marry a dragon from Eldavon. An arranged marriage."

"A political marriage," Herja corrected.

"It's the same thing," Wickham argued.

Herja winced. Yes, it really was. It was an arranged political match. Such a thing was almost unheard of here in Eldavon. Wickham wasn't the only one who had been muttering about how unsavory it was for a marriage to be arranged in such a way instead of the young queen falling in love with whomever she was to marry.

"Odentia is the only kingdom that this drought hasn't hit," Penelope said slowly. "So I understand that part, with Odentia wanting to ally with Eldavon to be stronger against the other kingdoms that might want to invade them."

"It's still an arranged marriage," Wickham said. He squeezed Herja's hand a little tighter. "Couldn't they think of any other way to make an alliance?"

"She's supposed to marry my cousin Hector," Kaia said.

Herja turned to her, eager for more information. "And he's all right with it? I mean, he has a fated mate, doesn't he?"

"Not anymore. She got sick and passed a few years ago," Kaia said, shaking her head. She stood and walked to the window, staring out at the landscape. "He and I talked about it a lot. He found the concept to be alien at first, but he's happy to marry Rowena for Eldavon's sake. They've been officially courting for a few months, and he's genuinely fond of her."

However, Herja could still hear the current of unease in Kaia's tone.

Wickham wasn't the only one who was opposed to this marriage. People worried that Eldavon was too reliant on Odentia. Others were worried it was all an excuse and Odentia would use the marriage to control Eldavon.

"Row is good friends with Lantos," she said. "Er—King Lantos. We visited with him over the summer. It might seem strange to us, but this is the strongest form of alliance that the other kingdoms will acknowledge."

"But isn't that just the problem?" Wickham demanded. "It's an alliance, not a marriage, but they're being married to each other all the same. I mean, imagine it was any of us. I can't imagine getting married without loving my wife."

"It's not us, though," Kaia argued. "It's Hector and Rowena. A political marriage, yeah, but one that they're both going into with eyes wide open. It's not our place to judge the situation."

Wickham slumped back. "I think I can judge the situation when they're being forced into a marriage. I'm allowed not to like it."

"They're not being forced, though," Kaia said, turning again. "I know. I've talked with both of them. Rowena invited me to the Odentian palace again this summer, so Nolen and I went. I was the one that brought the official contract back to Eldavon."

Wickham opened his mouth, then lowered his head. "Sorry."

"The marriage was Rowena's idea, and she asked Hector. He

agreed. Not without doubts, no, but he still agreed. Either could back out," Kaia said, straightening.

"Can they, or would it cause further trouble?" Penelope asked.

"They can back out," Kaia repeated. "That is something both of them agreed on before they even decided to get married. When I talked to Rowena about it, she looked forward to the marriage. She's fond of Hector."

Odentia and Eldavon striking an alliance that the other kingdoms would respect would help with the situation. Herja still regretted bringing up the entire conversation. Yes, she wanted to be aware of what was happening, and it wasn't as though she would get that information without talking about it.

But Wickham looked more tense and miserable than ever. She should have asked everyone if they were in the right mind space for this before talking about it.

"I think we've talked enough," Raven said suddenly from where they sat. "At this point, we're only going to run around in circles. It's been a long day—does anyone else feel like swimming?"

"I do," Kaia said. She headed for her bedroom door. "I'll get my swimsuit. Anyone else coming?"

Penelope nodded, and Herja pushed her hair behind her ear. "I think I'll sit out. I'd like to get a head start on the readings that Professor Underwood has assigned. We are going to have a lot of work to get done this year."

"I'll stay, too," Wickham said. "I wanted to get a few essays written for when I start medical school again. I tried to do long-distance learning, but they said I needed to concentrate on finishing up the Institute, and then I could dedicate myself to medicine."

He made a face. Herja laughed and leaned across to kiss him on the cheek. "They're right. You need to finish up with your magical training, and you'll be able to learn more efficiently then."

"Yeah, but I want to do both."

Herja stood and took his hand. "Let's get you started on your work for Professor Carmilla, then. If you get it out of the way, you can start studying for the medical midterms, then."

Everyone dispersed. Herja squeezed Wickham's hand as they got their schoolwork. It was a pleasant distraction from the heaviness weighing down on them—the threat of war. Herja could only hope that the measures the Crown was taking would be effective.

But an icy ball of fear in her belly wondered what would happen if it were not.

CHAPTER
TWO

The first week of classes was brutal. Kaia stretched her arms over her head as she and Nolen headed for the library to study.

"I didn't know there would be so much reading in this final year," she grumbled. Nolen carried her book bag for her and she eyed the heavy bag wearily. "I love reading, but this just seems like too much. We've always been more into practical learning."

Nolen shrugged. "Normally, you have a quest, too, instead of spending the entire school year here at the Institute."

Kaia sighed. That was true. But now all the witches had everything they needed to complete their spell books, so all that was left was the book learning and putting together the book. That wouldn't happen until the end of the year, though.

She turned when she heard her name being called to see Row, or Professor Farrow, approaching. Ever since Row and their mate had adopted Herja, their relationship with the fifth-year group had grown much more casual.

"The headmasters want to see the two of you in their office," Row said.

Kaia's eyes widened. Why would the headmasters want to see them? "Er... but we haven't broken any rules."

Row smiled gently, though it was still strained. "You're not in trouble, Kaia."

"Are you sure?"

This time Row laughed aloud. "I'm sure. Come on."

They gestured to follow and trotted off back down the hallway. Kaia grabbed Nolen's hand for support and hurried after them. Her mind whirled—what did the headmasters want to see the two of them about? It better not be because of that stunt that Lyra, a mermaid queen, pulled last year. While she was holding the students hostage, she arranged a marriage between Kaia and Nolen to distract them from what was really going on.

Kaia wasn't ready to get married. Not by a long shot. She was happy with where her relationship with Nolen stood right now—fated mates and best friends, with marriage somewhere in the distant future.

They got to the headmasters' office and followed Row in. Kaia's stomach plummeted. Not only were Headmasters Twila and Valiant there, but the dragon King Lantos, the witch Queen Johanna, and the human King and Queen, Sydney and Abigail. Even Queen Charlize, and she was retired!

"Oh," Kaia breathed. "There's so many of you..."

Nolen slid his arm protectively around Kaia's waist. "What's going on?"

Row bowed and slipped out of the room, shutting the door behind themself.

Kaia twisted her hands as she focused on Charlize. With her parents in the government, she had got to know the queen well over the years. "Are you sick?"

"No," Charlize replied with a slight shake of her head. "I'm here for moral support. I didn't want you to end up feeling overwhelmed."

She smiled and winked at Kaia, and Kaia felt a little better. She took a deep breath and faced the current kings and queens—remembering she really ought to curtsy belatedly, but it was a bit late.

King Lantos cleared his throat. "I'm afraid we bring some grim news. You know that Queen Rowena and your cousin Hector will be married here in Eldavon in three weeks' time."

Kaia nodded.

"Queen Rowena has gone missing. We got the news mind-to-mind with the dragon-witch guard accompanying her, her uncle, and her party to the palace. They're in the woods bordering our kingdoms and she has simply... disappeared."

"Disappeared?" Nolen repeated. "No. That's not possible. People don't disappear."

King Lantos focused on him, his expression showing no sign of irritation if he thought the statement was impertinent. "That's exactly why we are so concerned."

Nolen dropped his head, grimacing.

"Was she kidnapped?" Kaia asked, squeezing Nolen's hand. Her heart beat harder like she already knew why she was here—when, in actuality, she did not know. Why would the kings and queens come to the Institute just to tell her and Nolen this in person?

"We don't know," Queen Abigail said, shaking her head. "The reports are just that she disappeared. The procession wasn't attacked. She wasn't even left alone to be attacked, so we don't know what happened."

Kaia rubbed her temples with her free hand, trying to process the information. Her skin grew cold as understanding grew ... if there was no queen, there was no marriage. No marriage, no alliance.

And that Rowena had disappeared en route to Eldavon was even more dicey. How many of Odentia's lords would consider this a deliberate attack on them? Would it open up the possibility of war between the two kingdoms again?

This was the last thing that they needed.

"But why am I here?" she asked, lifting her head again. "Why tell me?"

"We're getting to that," Queen Abigail said. "We're just trying to set the background for you first."

"According to her uncle, the young queen called for a stop because she was tired," Queen Johanna said. She folded her hands over her knee, looking impressively dressed in all red. It contrasted beautifully with her silver hair and her husband's all-black clothes.

"They set camp and Rowena and her attendants went into her tent."

Kaia nodded. So far, it has made sense.

Queen Johanna continued, "She went behind a partisan to change from her travel clothes, and that was the last anyone saw her."

Kaia blinked. "What?"

"She just disappeared," Johanna said, gesturing upward as though Rowena had become a plume of smoke. "There is no sign of anyone sneaking in or her sneaking out. There's just... nothing. She was there, and then she wasn't."

But that was impossible. There had to be some sign behind it, even if magic was used. Maybe something small and subtle that the attendants had overlooked because they weren't familiar with magic.

The Chameleon Sprites from the Golden Forest could create portals to take a person from one space to another and only left behind glittery power to show they had been there.

"Could it have been the sprites?" she asked.

"Doubtful," Lantos sighed. "They have no reason to do anything like this, and our people in the procession saw no evidence that the sprites had been there. We have no reason to think they would have interfered in this marriage."

Kaia nodded. No, it made little sense for the sprites to randomly kidnap Rowena. "But who would have wanted to kidnap her, then? Maybe the guards were bribed to look the other way? Maybe it wasn't a magical attack."

King Sydney shook his head. "Unfortunately, we know it is magical. There were no footprints around the tent and the area had just had rain, so everyone was leaving tracks in the mud. If she were whisked away, they would have needed magic to hide their tracks."

"Oh," Kaia mumbled.

"As for who could have taken her..." Queen Abigail sighed heavily. "We are unfortunate on that front as well. People throughout Eldavon, Odentia, and the other kingdoms don't want to see this marriage happen. All for different reasons, too."

Kaia thought of the discussion she and her friends had had on the first day of classes. "But nobody would kidnap her just because they were upset that it was an arranged marriage, would they?"

Nolen cleared his throat. "You must have a lot of more experienced people working on this. So, forgive my bluntness, but what does it have to do with us? Do you suspect Kaia and me of interfering?"

"Oh, of course not, dear boy," Charlize said, reaching out to pat his elbow. She shot a brief glare over her shoulder at the other rulers. "You're here because it was requested that you two join the search to find Rowena."

Kaia's jaw dropped. "What? Us?"

"I know, it's a surprise," Charlize said, her gaze serious. She seemed to have aged even more since the last time Kaia had seen her. Her stature was getting smaller, her shoulders more stooped, her hair more white. "And you do not have to agree. Understand that. *You do not have to agree.*"

Kaia stared at her in shock, only half aware of Nolen's confused grumblings. Why did Charlize seem so adamant about this? If she was directly asked, especially by the kings and queens, shouldn't she agree? It had to mean that she was uniquely poised to help the situation.

Although what she could do was beyond her. What unique gifts could she, a fifth-year student, actually have to help find a missing queen?

"Why?" she asked meekly. "Who asked?"

The queens glanced at the kings. At this point, Headmaster Twila stood from her chair. The two headmasters had been silent throughout all of this. Now, Twila gazed at them with serious silver eyes. Her expression was firm but sympathetic.

"You both have visited the queen before, and you are Hector's cousin," Twila explained. She folded her hands over her desk. "Odentia still doesn't trust us. And so far, they haven't allowed our people to fully investigate the scene since they are suspicious that the dragons and witches we sent to escort them might be behind it."

Kaia shivered.

"The queen's uncle is acting as her representative now, and since she knows and trusts you, he feels you will be a wonderful addition to the search. When we find Rowena, she will need to see faces she can trust. And that's you."

Nolen let out a shaky breath. "And I'm being asked to go not because of me but because I'm Kaia's mate. And I need to protect her."

"Something like that," King Lantos admitted, spreading his hands. "The situation will not be easy to navigate."

Kaia shook her head. It didn't matter. She wasn't going to just ignore the fact that she was specifically requested to help with this situation. She was going to help in any way that she could. Straightening, she dropped her arms to her sides.

"I'll go. When do I leave?" she said, keeping her expression neutral.

"Kaia," Charlize started.

"It's a good point," Kaia insisted. "Rowena knows me. I can't imagine how terrified she must be, wherever she is. It's only right that I help find her. Especially since she's marrying my cousin, it's my duty to aid Eldavon in any way I can, isn't it?"

"Yes, but that doesn't mean you have to decide right this moment," Charlize said with a frown.

Kaia shook her head. "No, it doesn't. But I've already made my decision. I want to help. I want to find her."

"I do as well," Nolen said. "The last thing we need is for the tensions between Eldavon and Odentia to strike up again when so many other tensions are simmering under the surface right now."

Kaia smiled gratefully at her mate. She could do this without him, and she knew that, but in all honesty, she didn't want to have to go without him.

Her mind raced over the possibilities. She'd ask the others to join, too. Rowena might not know them, but they'd all been through so much these last five years it seemed irresponsible somehow to go on a mission of this importance without them. Wickham's medical assistance, Penelope's leadership, Herja's knowledge, and Raven's insight are essential.

"Wait," Charlize cautioned. "You still need to know all the facts—such as who the queen's representative you would work with is."

Kaia opened her mouth to say it didn't matter, but she froze. They referred to Rowena's *uncle*. She had assumed it was one uncle that she hadn't met, but...

"Oh, no," she whispered.

King Lantos sighed. "The representative you would work with on this is Finnegan."

Oh no! The air seemed to disappear around her as her hands clenched. What was she going to do now?

CHAPTER
THREE

P enelope rested her chin on her hand, watching Raven as they trailed their finger along the page of the textbook they were reading. All around them were the supplies to make their spell book the two had gathered over the last year.

Returning to all those locations now at eighteen rather than so young in years past had been quite different. And she was glad they had done it—she and Raven were closer than ever now.

"You're looking pensive," Raven murmured.

Penelope glanced down at her own textbook. It was all about military strategy. Even though she had decided she would be in the military when she was thirteen and hadn't wavered from it, actually learning about it was difficult. Eldavon had clashed in battle with Odentia a few years ago but hadn't been involved in an outright war for decades.

"I'm just worried, I guess," she intoned. "I don't like what's happening. I wish I could just figure out a way to prevent it. I wish we could all band together and find a better way to deal with the drought."

Raven slid a bookmark between the pages of their textbook and shut it gently. "I know what you mean. This isn't a simple situation to be in, is it?"

Penelope shook her head. She wore her hair loose today and curled the ends around her fingers as she considered the situation. "Have you had any further dreams?"

"Just of empty fields and dying crops," Raven replied with a sigh.

It wasn't exactly very helpful.

A quick clip of heels made her look up. Kaia approached rapidly, leading Nolen, Herja, and Wickham. Penelope straightened at the torn, confused look on Kaia's face. Combined with the overly-serious expression that Nolen wore—more overly-serious than usual, even—it made her shut her book and pull out chairs for them.

Kaia slid into one chair and folded her arms over the table. "I'm in a quandary that can't wait and I need all of your help."

"What sort of quandary?" Penelope asked, her gaze flickering between Kaia and Nolen.

"That's what I'd like to know," Herja muttered. She scowled fiercely, but worry still shone from her eyes.

"It's... it's hard to say out loud," Kaia admitted.

Nolen slowly sank into the chair next to her. "Queen Rowena was kidnapped by apparently magical means, and Kaia and I have been specifically requested to join the search party."

Penelope straightened. "Kidnapped?"

"We don't know for sure she's kidnapped," Kaia amended. "But... that's what it looks like. And that's not the worst of it. Finnegan was accompanying her to Eldavon for the marriage. He's the one who asked for Nolen and me to join the search party. Finnegan, of all people!"

"Oh," Penelope whispered.

That would explain the quandary. Over the past five years—starting with their journey to the Silver Springs—Finnegan had caused trouble on three of them. He had outright attempted to kill Kaia once at the Silent Marshes. Since then, he hadn't acted as violently toward them...

Penelope glanced at Raven. Finnegan was the one that convinced them to go to the springs at Thunder Ridge, where they were turned from human to gorgon.

The six of them had barely stopped Finnegan from drinking from that spring, too. Raven and she had searched for a feather from the rocs that lived high on the mountaintops during the summer. They had talked with some ancient gorgons that gave the spring its magic.

Finally, Herja spoke. "My gut reaction when you said Rowena was kidnapped was to go help find her. But if Finnegan is there? How do we know he's not setting a trap?"

"My thoughts exactly," Nolen said grimly, rubbing Kaia's back lightly.

Kaia propped her head in her hands. "But everything else makes sense. She disappeared without a trace, but she knows me. If I go, then I'm someone from Eldavon who she can trust."

Penelope lifted her hand, and both Raven and Wickham talked at once. "We will not help at all if we're talking over each other and making this more chaotic than it is. Kaia, I need you to lift your head. Everyone who has something to say, please raise your hand and Kaia can call on you."

"That seems very professor-like," Herja grumbled but lifted her hand.

With a sigh, Kaia nodded at her.

"I want to know why Finnegan is being allowed back into Eldavon at all, considering what happened before," Herja said.

Wickham nodded with his hand in the air.

Kaia gestured at him. "Do you know if Rowena wanted him as part of her guard? If she's disappeared, I think we all know our top suspect... he'll be heir to the throne without her around, won't he?"

Penelope winced—that was true.

Kaia groaned, hiding her face again. "I don't know! I never inter-acted with him at the Odentian palace. Rowena referred to her uncle a bunch, but I thought there was another uncle. Apparently not, though. Her father and Finnegan were the only children their father had."

"It's okay," Nolen said, smoothing his hand down her back in longer strokes now.

Wickham hummed. "Then we have to consider why he'd ask specif-ically for you two, especially with his past hostility toward you."

"I don't know. We have to consider it at all," Nolen said stubbornly. "We don't have to go. The kings and queens were very clear about that."

The kings and queens? Penelope bit her tongue to prevent herself from demanding more information. Okay. So that showed that they were asked to go directly by the Crown. This was far more of an intense situation than she had at first thought.

"We don't have to go," Nolen repeated.

Everyone watched him as his expression fell.

"I think we do, though. Not because we're being forced to, but because we have to help. It might be our only option."

Kaia lifted her head again. "I feel the same way. But I did receive an official letter from Finnegan. Adina and Icarus did, too. They were all personalized apologies. So that counts for something, right?"

She looked around at the others with a desperate sort of look in her eye, like she was begging them to answer her with something that would shoo away all her worries.

Wickham and Penelope both lifted their hands.

Kaia groaned. "Okay, the hand thing isn't helping. I know you were trying to make it more orderly, but it's seriously *not*. I feel like I have to figure out who to call on and it's just making me feel even worse."

"Sorry," Penelope muttered, lowering her hand.

"Did Finnegan give reasons for wanting you to come help?" Wickham asked.

"That Rowena knows me and so I'm someone from Eldavon that she can trust—no mention of what he would get out of it, though," Kaia answered.

Penelope leaned forward. "Do you think that his apology to you was genuine? Is he still a threat to your well-being?"

Kaia shook her head slowly, her expression lost. "I don't know. I thought it was genuine but now I'm not sure. I don't know what to do. Will going and messing up spark more trouble between Eldavon and Odentia? Will staying here spark trouble? I just don't know."

The others debated the situation among themselves. The only one who said nothing was Raven. Penelope turned toward her mate, wishing once again that she could read their expression—but that would never happen.

"Do you have anything, Raven?" Herja asked. "Any dreams that could help?"

"No. But you all know that I have a different view of Finnegan than you do," Raven said slowly, their hands clasped together on the table.

Penelope nodded, encouraging them to continue.

Raven bowed their head. "I believe that Finnegan's affection for his brother was genuine. Whenever he talked about his family, I felt true love in his words. He told me about Rowena, too. I don't think he would put her in danger just to spite Eldavon."

That was good, at least.

"When Penelope and I were on our quest," they continued, speaking slowly, "we contacted the souls of past gorgons. They told us that magic was becoming imbalanced in the world. It seems to me like this has to be part of that imbalance. Right?"

They looked up, the uncertainly in their voice clear.

Penelope rolled her shoulders. The weather patterns being messed up and then this mysterious magical attack on Odentia's queen? It felt like something bad was happening.

"If Nolen and I go, will you all come with me?" Kaia asked, twisting her hands tighter together.

Nolen looked grim but glanced around, as though watching for their responses. "I can't ask Odele to come with me. Not when I know Adina would come with her. And Odele won't bring Adina anywhere near Finnegan."

"Understandable," Herja said as she dipped her head.

"It's not just because I want you all with me," Kaia said. "Obviously, I'll feel better if you are all with me and Nolen as backup in case Finnegan has something up his sleeve. But there's more. We have proven that we work well together and that with these situations, the more of us working together, the better results we've had."

Penelope nodded her agreement.

"We all have different skills we bring to these things," Kaia continued, and then she focused on Raven. "And your powers are especially useful. And... and I'm ashamed of it, but being able to turn Finnegan into stone if he tries to hurt us...."

Raven let out a shuddering breath. "I'm not sure I'd actually be able to. Not on purpose, at least."

Herja patted their hand. "There's been significant progress in the Crown figuring out how to turn the animals back into animals, rather than keeping them as stone," she said bracingly. "Row and I were talking about it yesterday. Apparently, as long as they're submerged in the Silver Springs up to their neck, they revert to normal."

"But as soon as they come out, they're stone again," Raven said bitterly. "And it only makes it worse. If they couldn't be turned back, they'd be dead. Instead, we know they're alive, trapped in that..."

Penelope moved her chair closer to Raven's and put her arm around them. "But think about what Kaia was saying. If Finnegan is plotting war between Eldavon and Odentia, which is worse? Letting him do it or trapping him in stone?"

Raven was silent.

"I'm sorry," Kaia whispered. "I just wanted to be open about everything rather than having secret thoughts that I sprang on you later."

Wickham brushed his fingers through his long hair, then sighed. "I don't like the idea of throwing it in with Finnegan. Trusting him feels wrong after everything he's put us through. But I don't really see how we have another option."

Herja sighed.

"I agree," Penelope said, rubbing Raven's back the same way Nolen was rubbing Kaia's. "I hate it, but it feels like we're amid a boiling pot, and I don't want to be the reason it runs over."

"We've learned a lot over the years," Herja said, tracing a pattern on the wood.

"We're stronger than we were before, even from two years ago," Kaia agreed.

Penelope nodded. "And if there's one thing we ought to have learned by now, it's that people can surprise you."

"I'm going," Kaia whispered.

"Me, too," Nolen said.

Penelope, Herja, and Wickham all nodded—they would all be leaving. Last of all, Raven bobbed their head. Penelope wanted to tell them they didn't have to do this, but it felt hollow. She didn't want to go—none of them did.

They had to for the good of Eldavon.

FOUR

Wickham checked over his medical supplies, making sure he had everything. Pain relief, sterilization, bandages, ointment, and herbs for tinctures or poultices.

Wickham had never been more prepared to be the de facto medic among their group. He'd already had eight months of direct medical training, equivalent to a full year's worth. He knew his herbs; he knew how to channel his magic to help heal others.

So why was he so nervous and feeling like he was underprepared?

With a sigh, he packed everything up. How could anyone feel prepared for this situation? It wasn't every day you went looking for the missing queen of a kingdom that had, until recently, been hostile to yours. Really, it would be weirder if he wasn't nervous... right?

His younger brother, Rhett, sat on the end of his bed, a scowl on his face. "I hoped that we'd actually be able to spend time together this year."

"We will when I get back," Wickham promised.

"Unless you're gone until the next semester again. Then I and the other dragons go to the Golden Forest with the witches. I'm going to get my fated mate this year, Wick. I wanted to talk to you about it. I don't know who mine is."

Worry streaked his boyish face. Wickham smiled; he remembered himself how intense the worry and excitement about fated mates were in their second year. Even though Rhett was only three years younger than him though, fifteen still felt like too young.

Was it too young for Herja and I to be paired together?

"The stars know who your mate is. The best thing you can do is to look at each of the witches and figure out why you'd make a perfect match with them. Think about what you can do for them rather than what they can do for you," Wickham advised, feeling rather wise.

Rhett only scowled and kicked his feet against the wooden floor.

"I know it's not what you wanted," Wickham said slowly as he finished packing away his medical supplies. He sat on the bed next to Rhett. "It's not what I wanted, either. Unfortunately, this isn't something that I can ignore."

"I know."

Wickham ruffled his brother's dark hair, the same color his own once was. A pang hit his stomach, but he carefully pushed it aside. This was for the good of Eldavon, and he couldn't exactly let his friends go without him, anyway.

"Will you take care of my window herb garden while I'm gone?" Wickham asked.

Rhett nodded seriously. "I'll check it every day."

Wickham hugged him tightly. "Look after yourself, Rhett. And I know it's a huge deal about your fated mate, but try to keep busy as much as you can. It's easier not to worry about that when your hands are working."

"Okay," Rhett muttered, not sounding convinced.

Gathering his pack, Wickham cast one more look over his space before he headed out to where the others were waiting. He wasn't used to this, deliberately chasing a quest that would have such huge stakes for the kingdom—more than just Eldavon, but for all the surrounding kingdoms, too.

The others were already waiting in the Institute's courtyard. Herja wordlessly held out her bookbag, and Wickham settled his pack inside it. The bookbag wasn't big enough to carry their supplies and all of them anymore.

It occurred to Wickham just how much they'd changed over the last five or six years, even in the last three years since they were Rhett's age. The boy he'd once been would never consider leaving his little brother anywhere to go to do this.

It made him sad to think about how young and naïve he'd once been. He wished he could go back and hug that kid and tell him it was okay, that he didn't have to carry so much weight on his shoulders.

"Are you ready?" Herja asked him.

He smiled back, fighting back his nerves. "As ready as ever. So. I guess we should get going, right?"

Herja looped her arm through his and pulled him close to her. She turned then to the headmasters and the kings and queens, who all looked at them with smiles that seemed rather sad and grim. Wickham didn't like those smiles, though he supposed the one that he'd given Rhett was going to have been very similar.

"Once more, if you don't want to go, you don't have to," King Lantos told them. The seriousness won out from his expression. "This is a lot to ask for from you, and we recognize that."

"We've made our decisions," Kaia replied, standing tall. She looked fierce and determined, and that made Wickham feel better.

They were going together. Yeah, they had never gone into a situation deliberately like this, but they had faced many situations similar to it before. They would make it through this one like they had made it through the others.

And it was going to be easier to deal with the danger because they were walking in with eyes wide open.

"Be safe," Headmaster Valiant advised. "Rely on each other. Trust your magic."

"We will," Penelope promised.

Their guide, a dragon with a scar down his face, took his dragon form, shifting into an armored beast that was bulky and covered in spikes and spines. One by one, Penelope, Herja, and Nolen took their forms as well. Wickham ducked under Penelope's turquoise wings as he scrambled up Herja's emerald-colored sides to secure himself on the saddle that sat on her amethyst back. Kaia scaled Nolen's steel-gray form just as quickly.

And then they were off.

The journey took one and a half days. Wickham's back and thighs ached from his long ride on Herja's back, and he felt relieved when they arrived at the Odentian camp.

That relief was short-lived as the dragons took their natural forms again. Two witches and two dragons greeted them, but along with them was...

"Hello, Prince Finnegan," Kaia greeted, her tone cool and unworried. She curtsied.

Wickham was amazed at how easily she could swallow her nerves.

Finnegan, dressed in a simple blue tunic paired with brown trousers, bowed toward them. "Thank you all for coming. I could understand if you didn't want to."

"Rowena is missing; how could we say no to helping find her?" Nolen replied, his voice flat.

Finnegan winced, his expression twisted with worry. It was strange to see that on his face—Wickham had only seen him smirking arrogantly or screaming in anger before.

The two dragons introduced themselves as Commanders Kiango and Saffron, while the witches were their mates, Hazel and Henri, who themselves were twins. Finnegan led the way to the queen's tent, explaining that it had been under guard; only the dragons and witches were permitted to enter it since Rowena had gone missing.

"I don't suppose you've had any dreams of her, Mx Raven?" he asked, his tone overly formal. He twisted his hands, and Penelope and Kaia entered the tent.

Raven shook their head and ducked into the tent. Wickham followed them.

I'm going to stay out here and ask questions, Herja said mind-to-mind to Wickham. *Let the others know, okay?*

Wickham sidled closer to the two girls, and whispered, "Herja's going to ask questions."

Next, he moved closer to Raven and told them the same thing. Raven nodded, distracted as their fingers brushed over the low frame of a bed. "She certainly travels lavishly."

Wickham hummed in agreement. The bed was a feather mattress set atop a frame, held together with hinges. It must be so that it would be easy to fold up and put away for traveling. Still, it looked very heavy, and there were enough pillows and blankets heaped on top to serve his entire family.

Whenever Kaia and Nolen talked about Rowena, they talked about her like she was a steady-headed person. Were they wrong?

The floor was carpeted in rugs, and a chest full of clothes stood at the end of the bed. The partisan where Rowena had disappeared was set up in the middle of the tent.

There was no way she could have slipped out without being seen.

He seems to be genuinely worried about her, Herja reported. *I think Raven's right. He loves his niece and wants her to be safe.*

Ask him if he has any suspects that would have done this—leave off the 'could have' for now and let's just focus on casting as wide a net as possible, so we can at least figure out a motive, Wickham suggested.

He heard Herja asking but tuned out Finnegan's answer—Herja would give them all a full report on the matter later.

After only a few minutes, it was clear that there was no way Rowena could have been kidnapped or slipped away without magic. Wickham's gut still said that Finnegan was somehow behind it, even if he seemed to be genuinely concerned. He could love Rowena and still have kidnapped her—to take the throne, to maneuver himself closer to magic, it didn't matter—and have every intention of returning her unharmed once he got what he wanted.

Wickham stepped into the area with the surrounding partisans. It was just big enough to change clothes. Her travel things still hung on one of the partisan walls, while one slipper and one muddy shoe were both sitting on the ground. Opposite feet.

He frowned as he caught sight of his own reflection. A small hand mirror was wedged in the pocket of her traveling gown. The glass was clear and perfectly formed, but it was the frame that caught his attention. It was made of obsidian, brittle and fragile looking. The edges were carved in elaborate, twisting patterns that reminded him of the portal mirror the students had used the previous year.

Carefully, he picked it up. "I think I might have found something," he said as he stepped out from the changing area.

Penelope, Kaia, and Raven joined him. He showed them the mirror, and each took it, inspecting it for themselves.

"What about it?" Penelope asked, lifting her head.

"Doesn't it look like the mirror from last year?" he pressed.

Kaia frowned as she turned it over to the back, then back to the front. "It reflects like a real mirror, though. Portal mirrors can't do that. The frame looks like a portal mirror, though. Maybe there's a portal beneath the actual mirror part?"

She scraped her fingernails along the edge, trying to catch something to lift the glass out. She frowned as her fingers slipped smoothly over it.

Wickham sighed. "So much for that idea," he grumbled.

"I'm not so sure," Kaia said, attempting it again. "This feels too smooth. I've never had a mirror that I can't catch something on the edges... I can't even feel these crevices at all, even though I can see them."

"So there's our clue," Penelope said.

"You think she was taken through a portal that this mirror created?" Raven asked. "But it's so small. How could she?"

Wickham shook his head, confused. "Kaia, keep it in your pouch. We don't want to accidentally break it."

Kaia nodded as she stowed the mirror in the pouch at her hip. She carried the wand Nolen had carved her in this pouch, too, and told them that over the summer had accidentally snapped it in half when she fell. Together they had fixed it, but ever since then, she kept protective spells on the pouch so as not to damage it again.

A sudden shout from outside made them all dash out. Kiango and Saffron had both taken their dragon forms. Dozens of guards raced toward a line of dirty men who charged at the camp.

Wickham's heart jumped to his throat. They were under attack!

CHAPTER

FIVE

P enelope let out a ball of fire, shooting it at the encroaching attackers. They stumbled back, crying out, then turned and fled. She loped after them, her claws digging huge tracks in the earth. Once they reached the treelines, they scattered. The Odentia warriors filtered through the bramble after them, but when Penelope took her human form to follow, a sharp whistle behind her pulled to a stop.

We're not about to engage; Raven told her mind-to-mind. *Leave it to the warriors.*

Penelope curled her hands into fists, but even as she did so, she understood the wisdom of it. After all, she was unarmed. What chance did she have against their attackers?

Reluctantly, and walking backward so her back was not exposed to the forest, Penelope returned to the cluster of tents. Wickham was already tending to a few wounded people, Kaia standing beside him with her wand drawn.

"Oof," Penelope grunted, tripping against some invisible barrier.

"Sorry," Kaia said, then pointed her wand to a faint glowing circle on the ground. "Thank you for your service."

The circle shimmered brighter, then faded away.

"What was that?" Herja demanded as she came in from the other side, glaring at the woods.

"Highwaymen, most likely," Kiango replied. He stood nearby with his hand on the hilt of his sword, his frown deep. "The royal procession is a rich target if they can get their hands on any of the goods, and they left as soon as they grabbed some supplies."

Finnegan jogged over, two warriors flanking him. "Commander. Were any of your people injured?"

Kiango shook his head. "No. Just these two Odentian guards."

He gestured to the men Wickham was tending to. Penelope pressed her lips together, carefully not looking at Finnegan as she reached out mind-to-mind to Kiango.

It's rather a coincidence that the procession was attacked just when we arrived from the Institute. Could he have set this up? She asked.

Kiango's eyes flashed to her and then back to Finnegan. "It's fortuitous that they didn't want to stay and fight."

And to Penelope. *You are here to help retrieve the queen, not to cast dispersions on her uncle. I understand your distrust; we will discuss this further, but the Crown has allowed him to return for a reason.*

Chastened, Penelope moved to her classmates, keeping an ear on the conversation between Kiango and Finnegan as they planned on how to track down their attackers. Highwaymen, huh? Penelope held back her suspicions, as Kiango was trained and had been with the procession for a while—she would wait to talk to the students before deciding.

"Kaia," she said in the meantime, drawing up to where Kaia stood between Nolen and Raven. "How are you doing for energy? I'd like to use that trick you have to light up the paths so we... or rather, so the warriors can follow the highwaymen back to their camp."

Kaia's lips pursed.

"Highwaymen?" Herja asked a sardonic note in her voice.

"Highwaymen," Penelope said firmly, casting her a significant look. She met the gaze of each of her friends to emphasize the importance. "Commander Kiango believes they are highwaymen. So we need to track them down and find out what connection they have with Queen Rowena's disappearance."

The back of her neck prickled, and she turned to find Kiango and Finnegan both watching her. Her cheeks bloomed with heat, but she held her chin straight as she met their gazes. Kiango seemed a little exasperated, while Finnegan wore a strange expression on his face. Frustrated somehow... or maybe... was that guilt?

Whatever it was, it disappeared when she gazed at him.

"What are you doing, Penelope?" Kiango asked, his voice flat.

"Kaia has a spell that she uses to light up the footsteps of the people we want to find," Penelope said, gesturing to Kaia. "I thought it would be a good thing to use so that we can find the camp of the highwaymen before they return there. Since they're going to want to shake the Odentian warriors."

Kiango's brow furrowed. "Can you do that?" he asked.

Kaia nodded.

"I've seen it work," Finnegan offered. "When we were at odds at Thunder Ridge. I'd say let them do it."

At this, Kiango's brow furrowed more deeply, but he nodded. "Very well. Kaia, are you willing to do this? It may put you in danger."

Kaia nodded eagerly. "Anything I can do to help."

The dragon still seemed a little uncertain but nodded again. He called over Hazel and Henri so they would stay with the other students to protect them in case of an attack, then gestured for Kaia, Penelope, and Nolen to come with him.

"If I tell you to leave, you will do so," he said seriously.

Penelope agreed. "Dragon form, fly away. Nolen, you're in charge of grabbing Kaia—no waiting for her to mount, just snatch her."

She made a hand gesture like scooping something up from the ground, and Nolen nodded in agreement.

"What about Finnegan?" Kaia looked over her shoulder, squinting at him. "Are you coming, too?"

Finnegan shook his head.

Kiango led them to the edge of the camp, where Kaia pointed her wand at the ground, thought a moment, then said, "Footsteps, foot-steps, back and forth. Backtrack, backtrack, where to go?"

A line of booted impressions lit up in a pale-yellow line. The group followed along with them while Kiango kept a hand on the hilt of his sword. Penelope wished she was armed. They had been training in defensive techniques ever since their second year, but none of them had weapons of their own.

"You must refer to the prince by his title," Kiango said once they were moving through the forest. Despite the rain that had come through only days ago, everything was dry and brittle. "Prince Finnegan or his Highness. Not by name alone."

Penelope glanced up at their warrior-dragon guard. "I'm pretty sure we've earned a little grace in that respect. Considering everything he put us through personally."

Kiango brought them to a halt and turned to her. His expression softened, and he sighed as he ran a hand over his hair. "I understand why you would think that. And normally, I would agree with you in this matter."

So he didn't like Finnegan, either.

"However, he is an official member of the royal family of Odentia, a kingdom with whom our alliance is extremely fragile. Regardless of personal feelings, you must do nothing to risk that alliance." Kiango looked from Penelope to Nolen and lastly to Kaia. "I am aware of the past between the six of you and the prince. But you agreed to be here. And so, you must act as though you are official ambassadors for Eldavon."

Penelope nodded reluctantly. "I will keep that in mind."

"Good."

They continued on, and after half an hour, they came to the edge of the trees. They emerged to be on the swell of a hill. The footsteps they'd been following disappeared, but they didn't have to look any further, though. The hill they stood on sloped gracefully to a low, flat area a few miles wide with a low river that ran through it.

Houses were arranged in a grid on one side, while the other was crossed with canals. The fields of crops were brown and dusty. At this time of year, they ought to be vibrant green.

"I don't understand," Kaia said. She pointed to the ground again. "Show us where the bandits came from."

The footsteps didn't light up again.

Penelope started forward, but Kiango caught her and pulled her back. "Wait."

The three students watched him as he searched the area, then he gestured for them to follow him. They did so. Penelope's heart plummeted to see that he still rested his hand on the hilt of his sword.

They were in Eldavon, though. These were their people. They weren't a threat... but where did the bandits come from, then?

<hr>

Kaia ran her fingers over the smooth wood of her wand as she chewed her lip. Something must have gone wrong with the spell. Why would it lead them here, to this sleepy little village? The weight of the mirror Wickham found pulled on the pouch at her hip, and she suddenly realized they'd forgotten to tell Kiango about it.

They'd have to remember to do that soon.

The commander led them to the first few buildings, where a group of people were weaving baskets. As they approached, the group fell silent and watched the approach with wide eyes.

"Hello," Kiango greeted, lifting his hand to wave. "I'm Kiango, and these are Penelope, Nolen, and Kaia."

A white-haired woman with a braid that dropped to her knees stood. "Welcome. I am Helga. You're all part of that Odentian procession that's been camped out in the forest for the last few days, aren't you? Why are you over there instead of taking rest here, where there're solid walls and hearty food?"

Kaia looked up at Kiango. Now that Helga had pointed it out, it was weird that the procession would choose to camp in the forest rather than coming to the village, only half an hour's walk away.

"We did not mean to camp this long; some of our people have fallen ill, and we didn't want to introduce any sickness to your village," Kiango replied. "However, we were wondering if you've seen anyone out of the ordinary of late. We've had a few supplies stolen."

Helga glanced at the others, who were weaving. One by one, they all shook their heads. Kaia couldn't help but think they were giving the group some rather wary glances.

"No one at all?" she asked.

"No. No one."

Kiango nodded. "Thank you. They're probably wandering bandits, then. Make sure you are being careful; is there anything we can do for you in the meantime?"

Helga smiled. "Nothing, thank you. Please, I don't mean to be rude, but we have gotten over an illness that has taken its toll on us all recently. We would prefer not to get whatever you have."

Kiango bowed to her. "Of course. We will take our leave."

He turned and headed back the way he came. Kaia oddly got goose-bumps over her arms as she followed him. It wasn't until they were in the forest that Nolen voiced what she hadn't realized.

"Where were the rest of their people?"

Kaia turned to him. "What?"

"There were only a dozen people there, weaving their baskets. Nobody was tending to the fields, fixing things. The village was practically empty," he said, his voice dour.

She shuddered. "You don't think our own people would have attacked the procession?"

Kiango sighed as he turned back to them. They were well in the trees now, shielding them from the view of the village. "This is not something to discuss aloud. Keep your guesses in your head. The Odentia warriors already suspect Eldavon of doing something to the queen."

Shock rippled through Kaia. "But that's impossible!"

"It's not impossible," Kiango replied, his voice lowering. "Nothing is impossible. But this situation? It cannot be based on supposition and suspicion. We point fingers at Odentia, they point fingers at us, and what solidified a friendly relationship explodes."

Penelope let out a heavy sigh. "And the bandits being tracked to an Eldavon village will only make the Odentia warriors more suspicious, then. And any actions they make, acting on those suspicions, will only make us more suspicious of Odentia."

"Especially as you already have a tense relationship with Prince Finnegan," Kiango agreed.

Was this the reason he'd asked for them? So that he could push them into some action, which he could then use to break the alliance between Odentia and Eldavon? Kaia opened her mouth, then closed it.

That kind of wild accusation was exactly the sort of thing they needed to avoid making.

But that didn't mean she thought it was any less likely.

CHAPTER

SIX

When the others returned, Kiango, Saffron, Hazel, and Henri all went into Finnegan's tent with the Odentia prince to have a council with him. Herja nervously waited to hear what the others had found out.

"The commander told us not to talk about it just yet," Penelope muttered.

By this time, the two injured Odentian warriors were patched up. The six students were in their tent, which had been set up just beside the warriors' tents.

"I've put up soundproofing," Kaia said, showing their walls. "Nobody's going to overhear us. We need to talk about this."

Herja's stomach clenched as she noted the clear worry on Kaia's face. This wasn't good. Kaia always wore her emotions on her sleeve, but this seemed to be beyond just them being attacked. Nolen pulled her into his lap and wrapped his arms around her waist while Penelope and Raven sat close to each other. Wickham was currently sprawled on his bedroll while Herja sat cross-legged next to him.

"What happened?" Wickham asked.

"The tracks led us to a village. An *Eldavon* village," Kaia said, twisting her hands into Nolen's. "There were some people around, but not enough. When I tried to make the footsteps come back to show us where they came from, they wouldn't."

Herja swallowed hard.

Wickham bolted upright. "Wait! Are you saying that those bandits were from Eldavon?"

"More than that," Penelope said grimly. "If people from Eldavon would attack the procession for supplies... magic was used to take Rowena. It only makes sense that someone from Eldavon would do it."

"No. A witch from Eldavon," Herja corrected, her blood chilled. "Or more than one. And if there are witches involved, their dragon mates will be, too."

She met Penelope's gaze, seeing that same fear in Penelope's eyes.

"But why?" Wickham blurted. "Why would..."

"I'm not convinced Finnegan is innocent in all of this," Nolen growled.

Penelope sighed. "Neither am I. But neither am I convinced that anyone from Eldavon would kidnap Rowena, either. There's so much missing. But the important thing to remember is that our presence here? Makes it even more of a boiling pot."

"Because we have an unpleasant history with Finnegan," Kaia explained.

Herja folded her arms, frowning.

"But he's the one who asked us here," Raven said.

Penelope shook her head. "I know. The six of us have to be extra careful, is all. We need to keep ourselves calm, collected, and above all —we can't make any sort of accusations or suggestions about his character. Unless it's mind-to-mind *in private,* we have to stay utterly above the board."

She looked over all of them to make sure they understood. Herja scowled, but she understood it. Finnegan—Prince Finnegan, his Highness—was the most powerful man in Odentia right now as the queen's uncle... the only heir to the throne.

They absolutely could not afford to offend him or make his people think he was in danger.

This is exactly why royal inheritance is a bad idea, she thought, uncomfortable.

"So what do we do?" Raven asked, their voice low and afraid.

Penelope took their hand in hers and brought it to her lips to kiss. "We manage the situation as best we can, I suppose. For the time being, let's concentrate on keeping things calm here. We'll wait for the commander to give us direction."

Herja hummed as she shifted positions, wrapping her arms around her legs. "In the meantime, I think it would be best if we use Kaia's sunshine."

"Wh-what?" Kaia spluttered. "My sunshine?"

"You're the one that brought us all together in the first place with your cheery smile," Herja pointed out. "If anyone's going to calm down the Odentian warriors' suspicions and make friends, it's you. Although..."

Nolen chuckled. "I should steer clear."

"As should I," Herja agreed. "Wick, Kaia, and Pen are our more personable people here. The rest of us should try to stay to ourselves a bit more."

Nolen hummed as he stroked his fingers through Kaia's hair. Herja was thankful for her relationship with Wickham, and how they could have casual moments like the one she saw, although they preferred to be more private.

"I will not be playing mediator," Penelope said, shaking her head. "I'm going to try my best to work with the commander and get us actual things we can do, other than just sitting around twiddling our thumbs."

"I'm planning on spending some time with the doctors and nurses from Odentia," Wickham said.

Kaia slipped from Nolen's lap. "Then I guess I better go spread sunshine around. I'll see you all later."

She strode from the tent and Herja leaned back against Wickham's side. So people from Eldavon might be attacking the Odentia procession. This was not good... not good at all.

Before Kaia talked with the Odentian warriors, she first dug through the rations the students brought and retrieved a bunch of the cookies she'd secretly packed. They were her favorite, apple, pear, and oatmeal. She took this box to the warriors, first heading to the two that had been injured.

"How are you feeling?" she asked as she approached. They had fresh bandages, one that was slightly off-white rather than the blindingly white ones Wickham had applied. The Odentian doctors must have changed them.

The two young men eyed her warily as she took a seat on a log near them. They were both sitting beneath a canvas that had been stretched between three trees.

"Er... we're all right," one of them said.

Kaia smiled. "My name's Kaia, by the way. What's yours?"

"Aaron," the same young man said. "And this is Paul."

"Nice to meet you both. I brought some cookies—I feel bad that you were both injured. Would you like some?"

Aaron squinted suspiciously at her, but Paul accepted three cookies and ate at once. Aaron accepted one and pretended to nibble at it. Kaia pretended she didn't see that he was faking.

"This is a pretty messed-up situation, isn't it?" she asked. Her mind turned to Herja's words. Her sunshine. What was that supposed to mean? She probably shouldn't think too much about it. "I know that Hector's got to be worried about the queen. I just don't get why anyone would do this."

Aaron snorted. "Hector. The Eldavon dragon that's meant to be our prince royal."

"Prince Royal?" Kaia asked, cocking her head. "But he's marrying the queen."

"Yes, *marrying* the queen. That doesn't give him the right to be a king," Aaron shot back. "I can just imagine that he's behind this. Making a grab for our throne, so he can take our resources—"

Paul elbowed him in the ribs, looking alarmed.

Kaia tried to smooth her expression, though she knew she must look shocked. "Hector's my cousin. He wouldn't do that."

"Ah. Well." Aaron shoved the cookie into his mouth and mumbled intelligibly around it.

Kaia picked out one cookie herself, shivering. "I can't blame you for thinking that way, though. I have only been to Odentia a couple of times myself, but it's a beautiful land. Harsh, though. Your previous king didn't seem too concerned about infrastructure."

Aaron stiffened. "What's that supposed to mean?"

So much for her sunshine, putting them more at ease. Paul was eyeing Aaron and her warily now, too.

"I mean... the wealth disparity," Kaia said. "And he kept manipulating Prince Finnegan to come here to Eldavon and try to steal magic. So I understand. Why would you trust us with the history between our kingdoms? Especially since it seems like Eldavon hordes its magic, and now, we're suffering a drought while Odentia is blossoming."

Aaron shifted, seemingly uncomfortable.

"But my parents work in agriculture—our food stores are enough to last. This is about preventing wars from breaking out. And hopefully making more alliances with the other kingdoms, so nobody has to starve to death."

"Prince Finnegan never tried to steal magic," Paul grumbled.

Kaia sighed. "Maybe steal is the wrong word. But I was part of the group of kids that he tried to kidnap under his brother's orders."

"That's not true."

Kaia opened her mouth, then shut it again. Was this exactly what she wasn't supposed to do?

A thought occurred to her, and she jumped to her feet and hurried away. She heard them grumble behind her, guessing that this only solidified their lies. But she knew exactly what to do... even though it seemed just a bit insane.

She found Finnegan with Commander Kiango and strode forward, forcing herself not to feel the slithers of suspicion.

"Kaia," Kiango said, straightening. "As I told Penelope, you need to stay out of this."

"Only no, I need to work on relieving the tensions in this camp between Eldavon and Odentia," Kaia replied. Then she winced. "Sorry. I didn't mean for that to be as rude as it was."

Kiango folded his arms. "What do you need?"

"Finnegan."

"Prince Finnegan," Kiango corrected.

Kaia sighed. "No. I need Finnegan. The Finnegan that tried to kidnap me and tried to kill me and all of that."

Finnegan flinched at her words, falling back half a step.

"I need you to come with me and tell Aaron and Paul that you really did all that," Kaia continued, putting her hands on her hips. Now that she herself was on the edge of adulthood, it became abundantly clear that Finnegan really wasn't that much older than her.

"Why?" Kiango demanded.

Kaia smiled. Despite her suspicions, there was one thing she was absolutely certain of in this situation. "So that we can both confirm that we care about Rowena deeply and that this alliance is for the good of both our kingdoms."

"I don't understand how bringing up my past mistakes will be helpful in that regard," Finnegan said slowly. "Although I am sorry for what I did."

"That's exactly why." Kaia held her hand out to him. "In Eldavon, we're taught to avoid violence. We're taught to serve others and have equality between our ranks. You know that. So come on. Let's go address the warriors together."

Finnegan frowned as Kiango folded his arms.

"I suppose... there are worse ideas," Finnegan said. He nodded toward her. "Lead the way."

＊＊＊

Penelope stretched her arms over her head as she followed along the same path that she and the others had taken earlier toward the village. Since Kaia and Finnegan were addressing both Eldavon and Odentian warriors to hopefully relieve the tension between the two camps,

Kiango had asked her to return to the village and ask for some simple supplies.

The warriors wouldn't be told that the bandits' trail had led to the village, and a young dragon asking for sewing needles would not bring a lot of attention. She might see or overhear something that Kiango would not.

It wasn't exactly her idea of a good time, but Kiango had trusted her with this.

Are you sure you're going to be okay alone? Raven asked.

Yes. And you're supposed to be trying to sleep, Penelope replied, trying to sound joking. Mind-to-mind was a bit too honest for that, though, and the truth of her nerves seeped through the bond.

Raven sent an image to her of a beautiful blue-tinged flower just opening to bloom. It was their method of reassuring her.

Penelope smiled and sent back an image of a dandelion.

She was just getting to the edge of the trees, on the top of the hill that led down to the village, when something glinting in the bushes caught her eye. She sent an image to Raven and, without waiting for a response, went to investigate.

Only a few feet off the path was a ring of wild rose bushes. From almost any angle, it would look like one solid bush, but as Penelope crouched, she saw a distinctive, arching opening. It was just big enough for a grown man to slip, though... more than big enough for her.

She crawled through the opening, finding that the interior of the bushes was wide and taller than she would expect. She sent another image to Raven. This place was plenty big enough for a dozen people to be inside... which was weird because it truly hadn't looked that large from the outside.

The source of the light soon became apparent. Sitting in the center of this odd, hollowed space was a hand mirror. It was the same shape and size as the one Wickham had found in Rowena's tent. The border was rimmed with the same coiled, elaborate pattern.

Penelope picked it up. Rather than the glass reflecting her face like the other one had, this one showed a murky, smoky darkness. She squinted. Was that a person's figure she saw in the swirling smoke?

Light erupted from the mirror, blinding her.

She cried out, dropping the mirror.

Cold crept over her skin. The sound of her own voice cut off and everything went black.

CHAPTER

SEVEN

K aia stood to collect the bowls of stew from the Odentia warriors. A few of them made protesting noises, but when she reassured them it was all right, they gave them up without a fight. The discussion had taken a lot longer than she had expected, but she felt as though they had gotten to a good place now.

We'll come clean up, Herja said. *You make sure everything's ready to be done.*

"Were there any more questions?" Kaia asked aloud as she put the dirty dishes in the same bin that they had been brought in.

The Odentian warriors exchanged glances, but nobody showed they had anything to ask. Most of the faces that looked up at her were quite appeased. Finnegan, sitting in a chair facing the group, stood.

"Thank you all for listening through this explanation," he said. "You are dismissed."

The warriors stood, saluted, and dispersed. A few of them came to help Kaia, but she waved them off. Herja and Nolen approached, both of them looking more relaxed than they had before.

Kaia was well aware of Finnegan's presence near her, his eyes on her. It made her want to curse him. She couldn't wait for Nolen to be here so she'd have an excuse to leave again. Her 'sunshine' could only last so long, and the last thing she wanted was to actually have a conversation with Finnegan.

"I don't think I've ever had such a frank discussion with my people before," he said eventually. "Thank you."

Kaia glanced over her shoulder at him and nodded once. Then she beamed at Nolen, stepping up to him. He took the bin of dishes from her and, without a word, arched his brow at her, asking if she was all right. She gave him a brief nod.

"I am sorry for what I put you through," Finnegan said softly.

Kaia turned back to him with a sigh. "I know. But you still put us through a lot of trauma and you can't expect that to go away. We're here for Rowena, and I sat through that with you because it was the best for our kingdoms. But I have to ask that you please don't start trying to be my friend."

Finnegan lifted his hands and stepped back. "Of course. My apologies."

Herja and Nolen flanked Kaia. Their presence bolstered her. As she gazed at Finnegan, she remembered the year when she spent every minute terrified he was going to come after her again. It wasn't fair. She'd been a child. She didn't deserve that terror...

But if what Rowena had told her was true, then Finnegan had once been a child going through what he didn't deserve, either. He was the victim of severe abuse by his brother.

She shook her head and turned back to the dishes. Rowena could forgive him for his actions. She could understand where he was coming from—but only after he'd given her an actual reason to forgive him. His guilt was truly not enough. He had to prove that he'd changed his behavior.

Suddenly, an image blasted into her head. She gasped, dropping the bin of dishes. Even before she fully understood what she was seeing, she'd turned, drawing her wand. Nolen sprang forward, tackling Finnegan aside as Herja charged toward the trees.

"Shield!" Kaia yelled. A wall of light sprang to life in front of her and something small and shiny bounced off it.

Shouts sounded from all around them. Odentian warriors drew

their weapons as they came at the students, having only seen Nolen knock Finnegan to the ground.

A spot in the trees, just above eye level, shimmered. Kaia stood with her wand still outstretched, her mouth hanging open as she desperately tried to think of a spell to help. Herja smoothly transitioned into her dragon form, snapping at that glimmering shade.

"What are you doing?" Finnegan yelled.

From the corner of her eye, she saw Nolen crouched over the prince; his stance spread in such a way that very little of Finnegan was exposed.

A cry sounded out as the warriors reached Kaia's shield, their swords drawn. Herja's head whipped around and a dark figure dangled from her teeth. They kicked and yelled. Something dropped from their hands as Herja flipped the figure over and dropped them from several feet. They landed with a thump on the ground.

Herja pinned them in place with one massive, clawed hand and growled. The glimmering was gone, and Kaia lowered her wand, letting the shield drop.

"Don't touch her," Nolen snarled as the warriors came at her.

He got to his feet, his head swiveling. The warriors surrounded him as well and pulled Finnegan to his feet, but Nolen didn't seem to notice. Kaia hurried to him and he put a protective arm around her.

"There's a dart there," Kaia said, pointing to the shiny metal thing lying on the grass. "And it looked like they dropped a blowgun or something."

One warrior grabbed her arm.

"Off," Finnegan ordered.

They released her, scowling.

Finnegan stooped and picked up the dart, then looked over to the figure Herja was pinning down. Then he looked back at Kaia and Nolen. "You just saved my life."

"It appears," Nolen replied grimly. "And Herja has the assassin still pinned down."

Kaia's mind whirled. Her heart stammered as Finnegan strode to where Herja still pinned the assassin. The warriors retrieved the blowgun, and she vaguely heard them discussing the type of deadly poison that had been on the dart.

What had just happened? It all went so fast she could hardly keep up. Her mind churned over everything, her eyes locked on the assassin as Nolen checked her over, making sure she wasn't hurt.

They had just stopped an assassination attempt. Nolen had seen the shimmer, recognized it as someone being hidden, and sent the image to her and Herja. They'd all reacted on instinct... or rather, Nolen's instinct. He'd somehow figured it out and let them know without words, either.

She gazed with new appreciation at her mate as he cupped her face. "Are you okay?"

"Shocked," she replied. "But I'm okay. Are you?"

"Uh, yeah. Maybe some scrapes. Nothing to worry about."

Kaia drew him in close, letting her eyes slide shut. Oh, this was... intense. Very intense. Her heart was still pounding. Someone had just tried to assassinate Finnegan. Maybe they had a point for not jumping to the conclusion he was part of this.

She buried her face in Nolen's shoulder and tried to breathe.

***

Herja waited until the Odentian warriors had bound the assassin before she retook her natural form. Adrenaline surged through her veins as she followed Finnegan, the warriors, and the bound assassin to the center of camp.

Saffron met them. Her eyes skimmed over everyone and widened. "What happened?"

"The Institute students just saved my life," Finnegan said. He gestured to his warriors, and they threw the assassin face-down into the dirt. "He was using magic to hide himself in the trees and took a shot at me. Can Hazel and Henri put up a protective barrier around the camp?"

"Yes," Saffron said.

Kaia, who was still leaning into Nolen, straightened. "I'll help."

"Thank you," Saffron said, nodding at her.

Herja linked to Wickham and quickly explained what was happening as Saffron headed off, Kaia and Nolen in tow. Kiango joined the group, and Wickham promised to assist the witches with the barrier and inform Raven, who was asleep in the tent.

That taken care of, Herja stepped up beside Kiango as Finnegan glared down at the assassin.

"Who sent you?" he demanded, sounding like the arrogant, violent prince she had first met.

The assassin flicked their head, trying to get the hair from their face. They had long, dark hair and a fury burning in their eyes that made Herja's arms develop goosebumps.

"I am one man who would serve the great queen Lyra," the assassin boasted. "Our queen was contacted by Eldavon's Crown for help to take you down."

Herja snorted. "That's a stupid lie."

Finnegan turned to her, narrowing his eyes. "Why do you say that?"

"Because mermaids and tritons have a very strict binary society," she said, spreading her hands. "Lyra has no men in her kingdom, and he just proclaimed himself to be a man."

The assassin scowled at her.

"Ah." Finnegan nodded. "And no assassin would so boldly proclaim his true purpose so easily, either."

"So, who really sent you?" Herja asked.

Kiango placed a hand on her shoulder. "Herja, return to your friends. This is not business for you to be involved with."

Herja frowned at him. What did he mean by that? She opened her mouth, but the assassin laughed. He shook his head again, his hair spilling over his face.

"A new world order is coming," the assassin said. "A new magic. Everything you thought you knew will burn to ash, and when the flames have been extinguished, the Sorcerer will rise like a phoenix and establish a new rein."

"What—" Herja started, but Kiango's hand tightened on her shoulder. He shot her a warning look, the same sort that Row gave her when they were in the Silent Marsh and they were approaching danger.

"Sorcerer?" Finnegan asked. "What Sorcerer?"

The assassin continued to laugh, and then suddenly cried out in pain. Blood stained the center of his chest, moving out in wide circles. Herja yelped in shock and the warriors dodged forward. Kiango got there first and ripped open the assassin's shirt—

A knife was lodged in his chest.

Herja stared in shock as the assassin's eyes rolled to the back of his head and he went limp and still.

"What just happened?" Finnegan breathed, sounding as alarmed and frightened as she felt.

Kiango shook his head, crouched near the body with shock written all over his face.

A chain lay across the assassin's neck. A pendant lay on the ground just beside his head, jarred there from when he fell. Herja almost couldn't point it out, still processing what she had just seen.

"Look," she said, pointing. Her hand shook. "His necklace."

Kiango picked it up.

The pendant was a small obsidian circle with a smooth face on one side. The edges were intricately carved with the same design of the mirror Wickham found in Rowena's tent.

"This looks familiar," Kiango said, standing. He frowned at it.

"It's a portal mirror. We found one in the tent. Only that one was a hand mirror. We didn't think it was actually a portal mirror because it's too small and it has a glass face but... but..."

Kiango caught her as the shock caught up and her knees buckled. He helped her down; the pendant still clutched in his hand.

Herja let out a shaky breath. "Someone sent the knife through a portal. Don't you see? That's how they kidnapped Rowena. It's magic. Someone is using magic to do all of this. What did he say? The Sorcerer? Who is that? Who's doing this?"

She gazed up at Kiango's face, hoping against hope that the commander would have an answer. The older dragon only stared back, as confused as she was.

Magic was at play. But was it coming from Eldavon? It was impossible. It couldn't be Eldavon. Who would do this? And all that talk about ashes... her mind passed over the unnaturally hot, dry seasons they had been having. Magic couldn't do that.

But it was the only explanation.

If it was someone in Eldavon doing this, the danger was even more deadly than any of them had supposed.

CHAPTER
EIGHT

The Odentian doctor, David, was a tall, thin man with wide brown eyes and hair that was so slick it almost looked painted on. Wickham had been showing him the various techniques he'd learned to wrap bandages for an hour now, and the doctor's expression hadn't changed. His eyes made him look permanently surprised, but the set of his mouth was unimpressed.

"I worked with the village herbalist for a few summers and then took on a job at the Institute's medical wing," Wickham explained to him. "It was just last year I started formal training."

David snorted. "I started my formal training when I was ten years old. What exactly do you think you can teach me?"

Wickham's brow furrowed as he looked at his work. "I thought we were doing this so you could teach me some stuff."

"Really?" This time, David's tone matched his eyes.

"I never thought that I could teach you anything."

David made an uncertain noise in his throat. Wickham wasn't sure what that was supposed to mean—he was still caught up because he'd have anything to teach a fully trained doctor. He opened his mouth to ask why that assumption was made when Herja's voice came to him.

I need you.

Wickham quickly packed his things up.

"And where are you going now?" the doctor asked, but even as he did so, the door to the tent opened.

The warrior who strode in looked urgent. "There was an assassination attempt against Prince Finnegan. You are needed at once."

The doctor's eyes bulged. He threw a look at Wickham that almost seemed suspicious before he grabbed his bag. As they hurried out, Wickham reached out to Herja again.

Where are you?

Main tent.

He let out a shaky breath.

David gave him a searching look. "Did you get some sort of premonition?"

"My mate's calling me; I didn't know about the prince." His gut churned—it couldn't be a coincidence that Herja called for him right before they got news about Finnegan. Had she been hurt in the attempt, too?

He reached out mind-to-mind, following the familiar path lines to the others. He could contact Nolen, Kaia, and Raven, but there was no answer from Penelope.

He reached the main tent at the same time as Raven. Kaia knelt next to Herja, and Nolen stood guard.

Wickham dropped to his knees near Herja. She threw her arms around him and buried her face into his chest.

Finnegan, Kiango, Saffron, Hazel, and Henri were all nearby; Finnegan explained what happened as David looked him over. Luckily, nobody had been hurt other than the assassin.

"Where's Penelope?" Raven asked.

Wickham looked up at them. "I wasn't able to get through."

Kiango glanced over at them. "She was going to the village to see if she could get some answers. What do you mean you can't get through?"

"Mind-to-mind. She's not answering." Wickham's arms tightened around Herja as a slither of fear raced down his throat.

Raven let out a shuddering breath. "I can't either. She feels like she's in a deep sleep... but I can't get through to her."

Herja let out a growl-grunt as she pushed herself to her feet. "Maybe she's just gone a little outside your range."

"*My* range?" Raven snapped back.

"I'll go look for her," Saffron said, her expression blank as she spun on her heel.

Raven hurried over and fell in step beside the dragon. "I'll go with you."

Saffron's expression shifted like she wasn't entirely easy with that, but the look disappeared as she nodded. The two of them headed out as David declared Finnegan unharmed. The prince posted several guards around his tent as Hazel and Henri placed wards over it.

"We should discuss our options," Kiango said, his attention on Finnegan.

"Of course. Let's talk." Finnegan gestured to the tent.

Kaia strode forward, and the other students fell in step behind her. Wickham thought it was right for all four of them to join the discussion until Penelope returned, considering Kaia, Nolen, and Herja had just saved Finnegan's life.

Kiango blocked them, looking exasperated. "You three are still children. This isn't a discussion for you."

"Yes, is it," Kaia replied, shaking her silver curls. "And we're not as much of children as you think. Not after everything we've been through."

"I asked them here for a reason. Let them come," Finnegan ordered.

Kiango sighed as he gestured them in. The four entered Finnegan's tent. It was more sparse than Wickham had expected. Rather than Rowena's spacious tent, this one was smaller and more practical. A folding table sat near the middle while a cot made up Finnegan's bed.

"The assassin was wearing this," Kiango said as he laid an obsidian pendant on the table. "I believe you also found something that looks like this?"

Kaia dug into her pouch and laid the mirror on the table. "We were going to tell you... then we were attacked, and I guess we all just got distracted. I'm sorry; we might have been able to prevent this."

"What are they?" Finnegan asked. "You said portal mirrors, but I've read up on them. They take a huge amount of grounding to a magical source to work, and the smaller they are, the harder it is to charge them."

"It just means they have to be connected to something hugely powerful," Herja replied. She seemed to get back to herself, although Wickham still watched her worriedly. Her fingers dug painfully into his hand, and he'd never seen her so shaken before.

Kaia flipped over both of the mirrors so their backs were to the group. "Magic is unbalanced in the world. That's why we're suffering this drought. And now... someone's doing it on purpose. But..."

Kiango picked up the mirror they'd found in Rowena's tent and called in Hazel. The two of them poured over it while Wickham kept one ear out for Raven. Time seemed to pass terribly slowly, but eventually, Hazel peeled the glass face off the mirror, revealing the same obsidian portal beneath.

We found another mirror, Raven reported suddenly, making Wickham jump *right where Penelope's footsteps stop.*

Kiango cocked his head, then said aloud, "Saffron and Raven are returning. They found another mirror."

"Whoever took Rowena took Penelope, too," Kaia said, her face pale.

"We don't know that," Finnegan protested.

Herja pressed her hands to the table. "We do. They followed her footsteps to the edge of the trees, and they disappeared right where the mirror was. We have to figure out how to activate these things—maybe we can find wherever they put Penelope and Raven."

Wickham glanced at Kiango. The dragon's expression was smooth, but there was something in his eyes. Like he was looking at them and seeing that they weren't, in fact, children as he'd thought.

Which was fine for Wickham. They were almost legal adults; there was no point in calling them children anymore.

"Is it going to be dangerous?" Finnegan asked.

Herja's lips twisted into something between a grin and a grimace. "It'll be more dangerous not to."

Kaia let out a deep breath, trying to calm her nerves.

By the time Saffron and Raven returned, they were ready. Hazel and Henri both protested Herja's idea, stating that they did not know how much energy it would take to fuel these tiny mirrors, but they were out of plans. Every day they waited, the less likely they would be to find Rowena unharmed.

"Are we all ready?" Herja asked, looking around.

Kaia nodded silently. Kidnapping Rowena was one thing; she understood how that made sense in a sick, twisted sort of way. Remove Rowena, and there was a power vacuum in her wake. If someone was doing this on purpose to 'burn down' what was here, then starting a war was the fastest way to do it.

But why take Penelope?

"All right. Let's try this, then," Herja said.

She joined hands with Wickham on one side, and Raven on the other. Raven reached out for Nolen's hand, and Nolen took it and Kaia's hands. Wickham held his hand to Hazel, who took it with a doubtful expression on her face. Henri, Kiango, and Saffron joined in, making the circle complete.

Kaia inhaled, exhaled, and reached out to connect them all. A myriad of thoughts washed through her, and she quickly compartmentalized so that only her own were the ones that she reached.

The group then focused on the single mirror they had on the table in the middle of their circle. A flicker of light passed over its dull face, then a sort of swirling, glittering image appeared.

Finnegan gasped, but Kaia ignored his presence. She concentrated, trying to imagine that swirling mist to clear.

In the center of the mist appeared a shock of red. It grew bolder, morphing into the same color as Penelope's hair. Excitement raced through Kaia—it was working!

Penelope, Raven called, and their voice sounded like a thunderstorm in Kaia's head. The older witches and dragons flinched. Evan Finnegan drew back. *Penelope, wake up.*

The mist faded, revealing the image of Penelope in a dark space. She seemed to glow, a shimmering light around her. Her arms were wrapped tightly around a sleeping, dark-haired girl. Rowena. Penelope's chin rested on her chest.

Penelope.

Penelope groaned.

Kaia's heart beat faster. She called out, too. *Penelope!*

The voices of their friends joined, calling out to her, begging her to wake up. Penelope twitched, her head raising. The light grew brighter, and Kaia felt something pushing back against her. She ground her teeth and shoved back. Nobody kept her from her friends!

Penelope, Raven called in a voice like the sea. *Come back to me.*

As though struggling from the deepest of sleep, Penelope lifted her head. "Raven?"

"Get them out," Finnegan said. "Get them out!"

But that light was growing brighter. The mist was forming again, and Kaia could feel their hold on the image slipping away.

"My magic—it's feeding something," Penelope groaned.

Where are you? Saffron asked urgently.

Penelope's head slumped back down to her chest, and the connection was broken. The mirror turned black and cold again. Kaia tried to push one last time, but the connection between her and the others faded away as well.

Dizziness rushed over her, and she sank to the ground. One by one, the others came down, too, too exhausted to fight it any longer.

"What happened?" Finnegan demanded. "Where are they? Bring it back! I saw Rowena; you could have brought her back!"

His voice grew increasingly loud, piercing through Kaia's eardrums. She groaned as she pressed her palms over her ears. "Not so loud."

"Why didn't you bring her back?" Finnegan roared.

"Because we couldn't," Kiango snapped.

Herja pressed her fingers to her temples. "We did what we could. At least we know they're both still alive."

Finnegan made a furious noise in his throat. "It's not enough."

"It's going to have to be," Kaia snarled. She had no strength to get back to her feet yet, but she glared with all her might at Finnegan. "We want them back, too. We did what we could for now—and we're one step closer to figuring out what's going on. We will get them back. But yelling at us isn't doing any good."

Finnegan glared back at her, then turned on his heel and left the tent without a word.

Worry ate at Herja's stomach as she wove between the older dragons, looking for her friends. Ever since their experiment with the mirror, Kiango had been calling for more help. Powerful magic protected the mirrors, but they still had no idea who was using them or why.

Finally, she came back to their tent, where she was relieved to see everyone there already.

"I've been looking all over for you," she complained as she threw herself onto her bed. "Why didn't anyone tell me you were all coming here?"

Wickham, who was lying on his stomach attempting to read, shook his head. "We weren't all coming here; we just happened to all be here."

"Oh. Sorry for snapping."

"It's okay," Nolen said. He and Kaia were sitting at the table with Raven, attempting to play cards.

At least, Herja assumed it was all attempts—she knew herself, and she wouldn't be able to do any of this with the weight of Penelope's disappearance hovering over her head.

"Are we going to talk about it, or is everyone wanting to try distraction?" Herja asked.

Raven folded her cards. "I want to talk about it."

"Me, too," Nolen said.

Kaia sighed but nodded. "I feel like there's no point, but I do want to talk about it, I suppose."

Wickham tossed aside his book and rolled into a sitting position.

"All right. So. We're getting more and more people coming in," Herja said, her hands tightening into fists. "And I don't know about you, but it looks to me like the Odentian warriors are getting more antsy and angry with the situation."

"I've noticed that, too," Kaia sighed. "Aaron and Paul keep brushing me off when I try to talk to them."

"Doctor David yelled at me earlier for putting some bandages away before he told me to," Wickham said. "He didn't want them. Just wanted me to not do anything unless he directly told me to do it."

Herja rubbed her eyes warily. She had been hoping that it really was just her imagination, but apparently not.

"We should bring this to Finnegan," Kaia said.

Herja nodded in agreement. No doubt, the Odentian warriors were feeling outnumbered and intimidated, and they deserved to have reassurances. However, even as she did so, Nolen grumbled.

"Since when did we decide he wasn't behind this? I thought he was still a suspect," he said, looking unhappy.

Kaia took his hand, her gaze soft. "I know you don't want to trust him in case he turns on us. But I have a gut feeling that he isn't behind this. He loves Rowena too much, and someone tried to kill him. I know that could have been a setup, but it doesn't feel like it is."

"I agree," Herja said, bobbing her head. "He seems genuine. I know I'm not the best at reading people, though, so I'm willing to hear anything to the contrary."

Wickham sighed as he stretched his long legs out in front of himself. "I can't tell either way. I still feel this fear in the pit of my stomach every time I see him. But I also get the taste of those awful weeds we had to eat in the Silent Marshes when we were running from him and his men. So I don't know."

Nolen passed a hand over his pale hair. "I don't really have a good reason for distrusting him other than what he's done in the past—I just don't like him. I don't care if he said he's 'sorry,' he still tried to kill Kaia once."

A heaviness sank into Herja's chest. Yes, that was true. He had. "But he also didn't hurt us when he could have on Thunder Ridge."

"And I'd argue that could have been as easily because he wanted something from us as it was that he reconsidered," Nolen said. He hesitated then and sighed. "Regardless. Sometimes we have to trust our gut, and Kaia is good at reading people."

"She is," Raven agreed.

Herja nodded. "It won't do us any good to run around in circles debating whether he is trustworthy. Let's work off the assumption that Kaia's gut instincts are correct, then. What do we do?"

"According to the older dragons and witches?" Wickham made a face. "We wait or head back to the Institute."

Herja scowled. The last thing she wanted to do was leave, but waiting around was just as bad. It was maddening to be in this situation. In the past, they would have just figured out their next steps and moved forward together. That wasn't so possible when dealing with all these older people who didn't see the students as capable.

"I'm going to look through the books I brought," Herja said, swinging off her bed again. "With any luck, I'll find something about the mirrors and what could power them."

Her statement was met with dull nods. Not much else they could do at this point.

Wickham picked up his book again but didn't open it. It wasn't as though he was reading, anyway.

Nolen got to his feet. "I can't just keep sitting around. I'm going to go see if we can be part of a tracking team looking for those bandits. Who wants to come with me?"

"Gladly," Wickham said, tossing aside his book. He quickly got to his feet.

Raven and Kaia elected to stay in the tent and help Herja see if she could find anything about the mirrors in her books. Wickham and Nolen headed out and quickly found one of the tracking groups. Nolen just stepped in to join them, and Wickham did as well—they weren't mentioned as the group set out, so Wickham assumed it was fine.

"Be careful as you track," the leader of the group said. "There is heavy magic in what we have found leading us in the wrong directions unless you see the signs of what are true tracks and what are not."

Wickham nodded though nobody else did. That must be why Kaia's spell led her, Kiango, and Penelope to the village.

Wickham glanced around the group as they moved through the forest. They were a mix of warriors from Odentia and Eldavon both. He couldn't help but catch the suspicious looks that both sides sent the other. It wasn't just on the Odentia warrior's part.

He winced. Herja was right. There was something more happening here than they knew... hopefully, if they could find these bandits, they would get answers about who took Rowena and Penelope and how to get them back.

These new tracks led them away from the village, deeper toward Odentia territory. The tension grew more intense in the group.

They found the camp after a half-day's worth of tracking. Or rather, the camp found them. As they were slipping through the forest, with no sign of life from anywhere, suddenly, a group of armed attackers leaped from the trees. They smashed into the backs of the warriors, and Wickham had to spin and duck to avoid the slash of a sword coming toward him.

Dragons took their dragon forms and shielded the humans and witches with their wings. Nolen stood protectively over Wickham, his steel-grey scales flashing in the bright sunlight. The attackers came at them from all sides, shouting and whooping.

One of the Odentia warriors fell, and a witch blasted back the person to attack them. Wickham dodged forward, Nolen still clinging to him, and set to work taking care of the fallen warrior's injury.

The fight didn't last long, although when looking back, Wickham would think it felt like forever. Their attackers were quickly subdued, and the Odentia warriors were quick to bind them. A few of the Odentia medics helped Wickham take care of the wounded—one woman had a deep gash across her belly, but Wickham had seen worse. The others only had minor injuries.

The leader of the trackers drew a wand and pointed it at one attacker, a short woman with dark hair. "Speak only truth."

The woman glared up at him.

"Who is your leader?" he asked.

"I lead this party," she boldly declared.

Nolen retook his natural form as the other dragons did the same, but they ringed the group, watching as though waiting for another attack.

Wickham grabbed a poultice from his medical bag and rubbed his hands over it, activating it with magic, then laid it across the injured warrior's stomach. Blood pooled up around his hands as she gasped in pain. He pressed both hands to her stomach.

"Sorry," he whispered to her. "This is going to hurt, but I promise you'll be okay."

The tracker kneeled beside the leader of the bandits. "Who put you up to this?"

"Nobody," the woman said, tossing her hair. "I did it myself."

Wickham closed his eyes, reaching into the wound mentally. He felt along the edges with magic, searching for the depth of the injuries. Her spleen had been injured. He wrapped it in a silent spell to prevent further damage and to help heal what was there, then slogged his way out. Her abdominal muscles were cut, but they would heal.

"...gave us magic, so we could trick the Eldavon witches," the bandit leader was saying. "We didn't hurt anyone. All we wanted was to put our queen into a better bargaining position. She should drink from your Silver Springs if she is marrying a dragon."

Wickham glanced up. The tracker held a bag, out of which he pulled various bottles which glowed with the distinct aura of magic. His gaze flickered to Nolen.

"I'm reporting back to Kaia, Herja, and Raven," Nolen told him.

"Thanks," Wickham said. He tried to push aside the discussion that the bandit leader was having with the tracker and focus on tending to his patient.

He wasn't doing a great job of it.

His hands trembled as he opened the sterile needle and thread to stitch together the injury so they could move her back to camp.

They didn't know that Rowena was missing. These bandits had tried to frame the village to make it seem like Eldavon had attacked the procession. But they didn't know about Rowena—they had nothing to do with that. So what was this? The Sorcerer that the assassin had mentioned? Who were they?

And if this sorcerer had magic...

Where did they get it from? Were they dealing with someone who had drunk from the Silver Springs? Went to the Institute? Or had they found another source of magic, like the springs on Thunder Ridge? Could they be from the sea?

What was going on?

He shook his head hard, pushing that aside. No. He would not start spiraling about that, not now. He had a job to complete.

Breathing out, he steadied his hands and finished stitching his patient together. Then, he washed quickly and gave her pain management. He only had willow bark with him, but he gave it a magical boost to hopefully ease her pain.

"I'm sorry I have nothing stronger for you," he said.

She nodded, closing her eyes. "I'll be fine. I've gone through worse."

Wickham glanced over to where the tracker was. He was now talking quietly with the leader of the Odentian warriors. Both looked like they wanted to punch the other.

This wasn't good. Whoever the sorcerer was... it looked like they were getting what they wanted.

CHAPTER

TEN

As soon as they were at camp, David told Wickham to go clean up and rest. Wickham tried to explain what he had done to help the wounded warrior, but the doctor wouldn't hear it.

Frustrated, Wickham stomped to the water barrels, where he scrubbed the blood off his hands and arms, then went to the students' tent. He ducked inside, finding Herja alone at the table with dozens of books strewn out all around her.

"Where are Kaia and Raven?" he asked.

Herja looked up. "They went to talk to Kiango. I think I've found something."

After the day he'd had, that was welcome news. Wickham sank into a chair across from Herja, groaning. His feet and shoulders ached from helping to carry the injured warriors back to back.

"Are you okay?" Herja asked, worry shining in her eyes. "Nolen said you were attacked."

Wickham mustered up a smile for her. "I'm fine. They didn't touch me at all, and it didn't last long."

Herja studied him a moment longer before she nodded. "I think I might have found what the portal mirrors are. I remembered reading something about mirrors like that, but it wasn't in any of my history

64

books. Finally, one of them mentioned the tales of gorgons, and it clicked."

"Gorgons?"

"Yeah. Different magics make portals differently. Like how when Lyra used her magic to redirect the portal mirror we went through, it was rough to go through. And the sprites, they have a different sort of magic altogether that makes portals with that sort of grounding framework."

Wickham winced to hear that. If different magics made portals different, then it had to be witch magic that made these. Which meant a witch had to be involved in the whole situation.

Herja paused in her explanation. Her expression faltered as she watched him. "What's wrong?"

"Because this just proves someone in Eldavon is involved in this, doesn't it?" he asked, keeping his voice low despite the protections Kaia had put into place. "So Eldavon isn't as good of a place as I thought."

"But that's not what it means at all."

Wickham leaned across the table. "You said that different magics make portals differently. This is a mirror portal, the sort that witches make."

"But it's not the sort that witches make. Witches have to have huge mirrors to ground the magic to make them work," Herja argued. "This is an entirely different magic. They weren't made by witches at all."

Wickham frowned, uncertain. "I don't get it."

Herja sighed. "Gorgons, Wick. Remember the pattern around the edges? How it's all coiled, like a snake?"

Wickham frowned, trying to picture the edges of the two mirrors he'd found. He had thought that they looked more like thin twisting ropes or branches, but now that Herja mentioned it, it could be snakes. He pulled the tie out of his braid and undid his hair as he nodded at Herja to continue.

"The old tales of gorgons are fragmented and fantastical," Herja said, turning the book in her hands around. "But there is one story in particular that I remembered. It was an ancient dragon king who was facing a war, and he went to a gorgon for a prophecy. The gorgon refused to foretell the dragon's future unless he brought back her mirror that the dragon's father had stolen."

"That's not much to go on."

Herja shook her head. "No. It's not. There are other stories about mirrors being portals to other places. It's the only lead I've had. I'm certain they're gorgon portal mirrors. Gorgon magic is very similar to witch magic. It makes sense that their portals would be like the ones witches made."

"All right, that makes sense," Wickham said slowly. "But what does it mean for us? I don't understand how it's going to change our situation at all."

"Because Raven's magic should be able to activate it."

"But we tried that already," Wickham argued. "Raven was with us. We barely got the mirror activated."

Herja sighed. "Wickham. They weren't the one who was directly trying to activate it. We could barely activate it because Raven's magic was so diluted. But if they're at the forefront of it? They will activate it."

"I...oh. Yeah. That makes sense." Wickham tugged harshly on his hair, angry at himself for not seeing it clearly.

Herja reached across the table. "You're tired, Wickham. You can't expect yourself to function at full capacity when you're tired."

Wickham nodded, but he was still annoyed at himself.

"Anyway, Kaia and Raven were going to tell Kiango," Herja said as she picked up the books. "With any luck, we'll have Penelope and Rowena back with us before you know it."

<hr />

Penelope fought against the mist weighing heavy against her mind. It invaded every sense, leaving her cold, with a strange, sticky feeling clinging to her skin, like she was caught in a web of dreams. But the dreams wouldn't come. It was only this mist, gray and dark like stone.

Something seemed to wrap around her wrists and tugged as though it was trying to pull her to her feet. The mist lay harder on her, though it had no weight of its own. The tugging grew more persistent. Voices echoed in the mist, too far away for her to know what they were saying.

They seemed to call, though. Penelope inhaled deeply, then held her breath because the mist invaded her lungs, too.

With all her strength, she willed herself to follow the tugging on her wrists. She moved through the mist and reached behind her to catch the girl. For a moment, they were stuck again, and Penelope was afraid she was going to have to leave the girl behind—

Then it was as though something broke free. They sprang forward, the mist swirling away from them as they rushed through the air. Blinding light made her cry out in pain; then she was tumbling over the ground. The air was unbearably hot and dry after that cool mist.

"Penelope!" a voice called above her.

She blinked and looked up. Kneeling over her was the most beautiful face she had ever seen. She knew it was, even though she couldn't quite make out the features she was seeing. Beautiful and beloved.

She blinked again. The blurred face slowly became more focused, the individual features fading away. To a solid blue-gray fabric, shadows are showing where a nose pressed against it. Warm hands pressed to Penelope's face.

"Raven," she moaned.

"I'm here," Raven answered. "You're safe."

And because Raven said so, Penelope believed it. Exhaustion weighed down on her, and she allowed herself to sink back to sleep, free of the mist at last.

She swayed gently from side to side. Penelope felt herself moving, but she was so cozy and had this blanket of safety wrapped so snug around her she was loath to wake, in case she found herself back in that horrible gray mist.

"Some of my advisors are against the marriage, but I can't imagine them doing anything like this," a low, honey-like voice said somewhere to the left of her.

"I don't think it would have been any of your advisors," Kaia's voice replied. "I just wish we knew what was happening."

Kaia. Kaia was here. Which meant...

Penelope opened one eye, praying to the sun. She saw its light. Relief washed over her as streams of golden brightness filled her gaze. She sat up, tossing off a blanket as she did so. Laughter bubbled in her throat.

"You're awake!" Kaia suddenly was there, hugging her.

Penelope hugged her back, squeezing tightly just to make sure that her friend was really, truly there. "What happened? Where are we?"

She glanced past Kaia to the dark-haired girl who sat on a low red velvet bench. They were in a carriage, Penelope realized. It was well-made, with cushioned seats. The bench she had been lying on was wide enough to be a little bed.

"You're in the Royal Carriage," the girl—well, more like a woman, she couldn't be more than a few years older than Penelope—said. "I'm Rowena, queen of Odentia. I must thank you, Penelope. If it weren't for you, I would still be in that horrid place."

Penelope shuddered. "It was just this empty place, Kaia. Filled with this glittering gray mist. It was awful. I found a mirror and—"

"And blinding light erupted from it," Rowena interrupted. "And then you were in that place. Until you woke up and were here."

Penelope nodded, shuddering again. She was glad Rowena had woken first, meaning that the young queen would have already explained what that place was like. Kaia finally released her hug and sat back on the bench.

"Nolen and Raven have flown ahead to the Eldavon palace with the mirrors," Kaia told her as Penelope's head turned toward the curtains. "They're powered by gorgon magic, and so far, only Raven's magic has controlled them at all. We didn't want to risk them activating again."

"Right." Penelope closed her eyes again. She was still so tired!

Kaia rubbed her back. "Are you okay? Do you need anything to eat or drink?"

Penelope shook her head. "I think I just need some time to wake up. I feel like I have the tail end of a sleeping spell on me."

"You do," Kaia replied grimly. "It was so powerful that it took all the witches to remove it. Rowena didn't have one, so I can only guess that whoever did this was afraid that you'd break free and not her."

"Any idea who that is?" Penelope asked.

Kaia shook her head, her expression rueful. "Unfortunately, no. Someone calling themself 'the sorcerer' but nothing more."

"The sorcerer," Penelope repeated. It seemed so nondescript, but goosebumps rose along her arms. She rubbed them, trying to act as though she was just chilled. "I think I remember hearing a voice. It sounded so distant, though. I don't know if I heard it or not."

"You did," Rowena said softly. "It was him. The sorcerer. I'm sure of it. And I'm sure if I heard his voice again, I'd recognize who he is."

Penelope shook her head, trying to push memories of the mist away. There would be time later. She realized she was squeezing Kaia's hand too tightly and loosened her grip. "So, are we heading for the palace?"

"Yes," Rowena answered. She grinned, though it seemed strained. "After all, despite everything that happened... I still have a wedding to attend."

"That's still happening?"

Rowena nodded. "The sorcerer is trying to stop the alliance between Odentia and Eldavon. I won't let that happen. This marriage is the best way to prevent it."

Penelope leaned back in her seat, too tired to do anything but accept it. The sorcerer. But who was he? And what was he planning next?

CHAPTER
ELEVEN

Herja rested against the wall, turning her face to the sky as she breathed in. They had arrived at the Eldavon palace just last night, and it had been a long night of telling the kings and queens what they had discovered. Today, it had been an early morning to help prepare for the royal wedding—Rowena had, at the last minute, asked all six of the students to be part of the wedding party as thanks for helping her.

"Not sure how this is supposed to be a reward," Herja muttered, although she knew it was—being involved in these sorts of things would be good for her future career, too, as she was building better connections to network with.

Footsteps sounded, and she looked up sharply, then relaxed when she saw it was Lantos. He and Row were good friends, and since Row had adopted her at the end of the last school year, she'd spent a lot of time with Lantos and Johanna. Using their royal titles felt almost too formal these days.

"Herja," he greeted with a slight nod toward her. "I thought I saw you come out here. I wanted to check on you, make sure you're doing all right."

"Yeah, I'm good," Herja said. "Just taking a bit of a breather before the wedding."

Lantos joined her, leaning against the wall. Herja was amused to see that they were similarly dressed in all black, although Lantos trimmed it with gold, and she had gone with silver.

"What's going to happen to the gorgon mirrors?" she asked.

"They're being kept in the vaults, being studied. You don't have to worry about it. We've got this taken care of."

Herja smiled wryly as she shook her head. "Yeah, that doesn't work. Not worrying about it. Just think about it, Lantos. The others and I have been through so much. We've already brokered truces and have had to act with the weight of the kingdom on our shoulders."

"I know," Lantos said slowly, a pucker in his brow.

"When we were at the Odentian camp, Kiango and the others treated us as though we were incapable when specifically asked there." Herja folded her arms as she sighed heavily. "It's been extremely frustrating. This was one of the first times we had older, more experienced people there to help us. And they acted like we were made of glass."

Lantos was quiet for a moment, and his head bowed slightly as though he was thinking about her words. Eventually, he looked back up. "You are all only eighteen."

"Raven's nineteen."

Lantos' lips twitched, though, in amusement or exasperation, Herja couldn't tell. "Nineteen isn't that much different from eighteen. It comes down to that here in Eldavon; we have difficulty seeing when kids become adults. Normally there are a lot more milestones that you'd pass before you get there."

Herja squinted at him. "So, you're saying that we are adults?"

"I'm not sure. But yes, you have gone through a lot that your peers haven't had to go through—and by that, I mean all your years at the Institute, as opposed to your human peers. Your experiences are more intense than many adults have faced," he continued. "And it's difficult to remember. That means you have different emotional intelligence."

Herja sighed. That was just another way of saying that they were still kids. Or at least in that awkward stage where they weren't still children but weren't adults yet. And no, they weren't adults in the strictest sense of the word.

The Crown covered their education, housing, and food costs. If they took out loans limited to a few thousand dollars, their interest rate wasn't allowed to be more than one percent. They could be married now but were cautioned against making lifelong commitments, even when the couple was a fated match pairing.

Eldavon took great pride in upholding systems to protect their young people from being taken advantage of. Herja knew that, despite the experiences she had with her classmates, they still had little life experiences that would allow them to thrive in society. But when it came to life and death situations? She was confident in her ability to handle those.

"I guess this is why Row was so insistent that I try to make human friends, too," Herja said with a shrug. "So, I can learn how to make small talk."

"Give me a political emergency any day," Lantos said urgently.

A clear voice called out to them. "There you are! You're going to be late."

Herja twisted to see Johanna, looking resplendent in all green, hurrying toward them. She pushed against the wall as Lantos did as well. He kissed his wife on the cheek, then wished Herja luck with her part in the wedding.

Luck. What was lucky was that all she would have to do was stand at the front and not do anything. She hadn't been to a wedding before.

She felt nervous about the wedding and uneasy about the secrets in Eldavon.

Kaia skipped after Hector and Rowena as they walked hand-in-hand out of the old Star Cathedral, where the wedding had occurred. The silver bangles that they wore—representing the star threads that now bound them together—clinked against each other as they smiled. They both looked so happy, Rowena leaning against Hector's side that didn't feel put on.

The reception would be held in the courtyard. Various people from all over Eldavon and Odentia would be there, although the dignitaries from other kingdoms had mostly elected to view the wedding and retire.

She hoped that the happiness beaming from Rowena and Hector's faces wasn't just them putting on a show. They looked happy. They looked like they might even be in love, and she desperately hoped that they were.

Outside, the clear autumn sky blazed blue and gold overhead. The perfect day to have a party outdoors. The orchestra played, and Kaia stretched her arms over her head. Standing through the ceremony had left her legs a little achy, but she knew once she moved, that would disappear.

Nolen wove his way through the crowd dressed in their best clothes. He grinned at her, his silver eyes soft and warm. As he approached, he held his hand out to her. "Care to dance?"

"Yes!" Kaia grasped his hand.

They moved to the dance floor at a dignified pace, then wrapped their arms around each other and waltzed. The line of well-wishers that Rowena and Hector would have to greet was a long one; they wouldn't be able to dance at all. Not that they were expected to.

"It was a beautiful wedding," Kaia said as she and Nolen kept their steps timed perfectly. "All the color and then their vows. They look good together. Happy."

Nolen nodded. "They do. All this is making me think about what our wedding will be like."

Kaia laughed. "Yeah, me too. I have so many ideas about what I want, and few of them can even go together. And that's without even asking you what your ideas are. But... do you even want a wedding? It's so much of being the center of attention."

"I want a wedding. Not this big, but I want to see you as the center of attention. I want you to be celebrated," Nolen said, then cocked his head to one side and grinned. "Besides, I think I'm getting a lot better at navigating your family."

"You are," Kaia reassured him.

They both lapsed into silence, remembering the first disastrous time Nolen met her family. She had utterly overwhelmed him with her unspoken expectations and the sheer amount of family she had. He hadn't handled it well, and it had caused them both to question themselves. They had both learned how to communicate with each other so much better since that time.

"I don't want you to have an uncomfortable wedding, though," Kaia said. Their dancing was slowing, though they kept out of the way of other waltzing couples. "It's something I'm completely willing to compromise on."

Nolen shrugged. "I would be happy with an official binding ceremony with only our parents, Odele, Herja, Penelope, Wickham, and Raven. But you're going to want all your aunts, uncles, cousins, Madam Adora... I don't want to take that from you."

"A compromise," Kaia said slowly.

Nolen gave her a wry smile. "A compromise in that we can just invite all family?"

"That's not what I was thinking, no," she said, shaking her head. "Even with just my side of the family, it makes it far too big for your comfort levels."

"I'm not sure what sort of compromise we can have, then."

Kaia's brow wrinkled. "Maybe we need to have two ceremonies, then. One for you and one for me."

Nolen snickered. "How would that work?"

"When we decide to marry, we can have the official binding first and ask that it not be made a big deal out of right away. We can have a small and simple event and then plan a bigger wedding for our five-year anniversary.

Nolen's expression turned thoughtful. "I suppose that might work. Although we could also have the official binding be a small, intimate ceremony and then have a larger reception a few months later instead, so you're not waiting so long."

"I can handle it," Kaia replied a little dryly. "Especially as I'm not sure what sort of budget I should look at. I would rather spend our money on giving ourselves a good start in life, rather than on a party. Five years of working and building special savings for it will be good."

Nolen smiled, his eyes glowing with such light that it took her breath away. "I love you."

"I love you, too."

They beamed at each other. Kaia lifted her face, pressing herself to her toes—

"Kaia," Wickham said.

Kaia jumped. She turned, annoyed, but when she saw the stress lines on Wickham's face, her heart dropped. His jaw was clenched tight, and he kept shooting nervous looks around at the others.

"What is it?" Nolen asked, his expression hardening.

"Finnegan has disappeared. Raven noticed he was not anywhere, and no one could remember when he was last seen." Wickham's eyes shone with worry as he shot them both a significant look, then tilted his head toward Eldavon Mountain.

Kaia's lungs drained of air. He wouldn't... after everything that had happened, Finnegan had learned his lesson about trying to take magic for himself, hadn't he?

Nolen put his arm around her waist, and the three of them hurried into the palace, where Herja, Penelope, and Raven were waiting. Herja and Penelope looked stressed, though Kaia couldn't tell what they felt about Raven's body language.

"There's no sign of Finnegan anywhere," Penelope said. "I'm certain he's gone for the Silver Springs. He wasn't at the wedding."

"But it takes three days to get to the top of the mountain," Kaia said, hoping. That meant they had enough time to go after him and stop him.

Herja shook her head. "The paths were cut to be a gentle gradient for thirteen-year-olds with late morning starts and waypoints they stop at every night. Cutting directly up the mountainside wouldn't take over seven or eight hours of climbing."

Kaia's stomach churned. "And how long to fly?"

"I don't know," Herja said. "But we can't interrupt the party. This might cause more trouble between Eldavon and Odentia—"

"Let's go," Nolen interrupted, striding toward the far side of the palace. "We can talk on the way."

CHAPTER
TWELVE

Penelope dropped near the small stone building that held the sacred Silver Springs. Raven slid off her back, and Penelope retook her natural form. They dashed toward the small stone building that housed the springs, crowding in behind the two of them.

The door was open, and Penelope rushed in, then came to a sudden stop. Finnegan kneeled beside the spring. He wore the same clothes that he had been wearing when they came in the previous night. A cup was in his hand, water dripping from it.

He already drank.

"Finnegan," Kaia started but fell silent again.

The six of them stood there, watching silently. Penelope's mind raced. They were too late; they couldn't stop him. Maybe he'd gotten permission from the Crown. Or they had decided he'd changed enough to be worthy of drinking. Maybe it was part of the marriage because Hector was Rowena's husband now, but he couldn't be the only dragon in Odentia...

Finnegan got to his feet, his back to them, and placed the cup back in its small cubbyhole on the wall. He stretched his back as he rubbed his neck. He had to know that they were all there, but he didn't make any sign that he did.

Pale light trickled through the tinted windows that were situated atop the stone building. It cast colorful images about it. Finnegan's hair looked almost silver. Not as pure silver as Kaia or Wickham's, but Penelope couldn't tell if it was just the light or his hair had actually changed color. If he was a witch, what would happen next? She couldn't imagine him willingly going through the training that the children went through.

"So. Does Eldavon have punishments for those who drink from the Silver Springs without permission?" he asked without turning.

Penelope expected Herja or Kaia to answer, but the silence stretched on. Finally, she could no longer stand the silence, and so came forward slowly, not knowing what the consequences of this would be in the immediate time.

"I'm not sure exactly what the laws are," she said, "but this place is sacred. You've violated the kingdom's most holy place. Do you really think it will be without punishment?"

Finnegan lifted it on the shoulder and dropped it. "You have been extremely merciful to this point. Now where's a mirror? I need to see."

"You're really taking this so lightly?" Penelope seethed, anger building in her chest. "Has it ever occurred to you that the mercy you've been shown was because we could see the abuse you went through at the hand of your brother, and we wanted to show you a way to be better?"

Raven laid their hand on Penelope's arm, bringing her to a stop. Penelope took a deep breath, forcing herself to think through this. She didn't want to cause more trouble when they had already barely made it out of these latest events.

Magic was unbalanced in the world. Which meant that something was wrong... and the sorcerer, whoever they were, had already targeted Odentia. Maybe it would be a good thing for Finnegan to have magic, then. Maybe it would open the doors to people from other kingdoms working with Eldavon. Somehow. She wasn't sure she could exactly believe it, but there was no point in blowing up here.

She didn't have the authority to punish Finnegan.

Finnegan's actions couldn't make the unbalance of magic worse, right?

"There's a mirror at the end of the room," Raven said, pointing though Finnegan kept his back to them. "It's covered by that green cloth."

The mirror stood in a clear block of sunshine. Finnegan strode to it and pulled the cloth off from over it. Penelope held her breath as the mirror reflected the light, filling the entire room with a new light.

Finnegan stepped in front of the mirror. His reflection bounced back to them, and Penelope waited, her heart beating shallowly.

With the new light, Penelope saw his hair was still dark. So not a witch. His eyes bored into his own reflection as she and the others moved forward. She held her breath as she searched these eyes; the closer she got, the clearer they became. Still, the same dark blue that they had always been.

He was human. He had the magic of the earth in him. Penelope's shoulders slumped forward, a sigh whistling from her lungs. Human magic was far more subtle than witch or dragon, and in that subtly, he wouldn't see the difference in himself. Not yet, at least.

"That's it?" Finnegan asked. He sounded frustrated, disbelieving. "After all this time, and there's nothing?"

He turned to glare at the small stream bubbling in the pool area of the building. His hands clenched, and Penelope eyed him warily. Would he have one of his explosive bouts of temper like they had witnessed in the past?

She should say something. But what? She didn't have the empathy to console him for not getting the results he wanted when he stole a drink from the Silver Springs.

Raven stepped forward, striding toward Finnegan. "Do you know what Eldavon says about the three branches of magic?"

"Three?" Finnegan turned to them, brow furrowed.

"Three," Raven repeated. They put a hand on Finnegan's shoulder and gently guided them toward the back door; the rest of the students followed.

Penelope glanced around, seeing the same confusion and anger on her friends' faces as she struggled with herself. She kept quiet, though, not wanting to make it worse; Raven talked quietly, explaining how in the Eldavon tales, dragons were created as protectors, witches as helpers, and humans as balancers.

Balance, Penelope thought, shaking her head. *Does the world's magic being unbalanced mean that we aren't listening to humans enough?*

The day was hot and bright outside. Penelope turned her face to the sun and closed her eyes, breathing in the dance of warmth across her skin.

"Dragons get their light from the sun," Raven explained as they led the way to the path that went down the mountain. "Witches from the moon. Humans have earth magic. They are vital to the health of our lives. It's why we have two human rulers, while only one dragon and one witch."

Finnegan's shoulders slumped, and Penelope wondered how much he was actually listening.

"Shouldn't we fly back down?" Kaia whispered.

"I think it might be best to keep Finnegan away from everyone else for the time being," Penelope whispered back. "But you and Nolen should go on ahead to tell the Crown what happened, so they can be ready to deal with the situation."

Nolen nodded, but Herja caught his arm. "Go to the other side of the mountain and take your dragon form there. I don't think it's a good idea to show Finnegan what we're doing right away."

"He'll figure it out," Wickham argued.

Penelope shook her head. "I agree with Herja. He's obviously disappointed, and I don't want to risk him having a breakdown or taking off to avoid getting punished."

Wickham nodded once.

Kaia and Nolen split from the group. Then Herja, Wickham, and Penelope hurried to catch up with Raven and Finnegan. Raven was still explaining the role of humans in their world. Penelope hoped they could get through the Finnegan...

And hoped this meant Finnegan had a role in restoring balance as well.

Wickham stood in the corner with Herja as the four others sat on a wide couch facing Rowena.

They had taken the path down the mountain with frequent mind-to-mind check-ins with Nolen and Kaia, who were at the palace. It'd taken them two days, but everyone agreed that would be the best action. The Crown didn't want it widespread that Finnegan had gone to the Springs and drank from it without permission until they came to an agreement with Rowena on what would be done.

As soon as they returned to the palace, Finnegan was placed under house arrest. Wickham wasn't sure what discussions the kings and queens had with Rowena behind closed doors. But after another day of celebrating the marriage, Rowena asked the six students to meet her in her room.

"Thank you for seeing me," Rowena said. She glanced up at Wickham and Herja, an uncertain look on her face.

"My social energy is very low right now," Herja explained. "I need a bit of extra space right now."

Rowena nodded, then smoothed her skirt down with her hand. "I just wanted to thank you all for handling the situation with such... discretion. After careful consideration, the kings and queens of Eldavon have agreed that I should take my uncle back to Odentia rather than leave him to be imprisoned here. He will be forever barred from returning to Eldavon, however."

Wickham nodded once, fighting to keep his expression blank. It somehow didn't seem like enough of a punishment to him... but he supposed there were plenty of political reasons to hand him over to his niece like this.

Still, after everything Finnegan had done, his drinking from the Springs proved that, at the core, he hadn't changed. He had no intention of changing, either. That much was clear. His motivations might have shifted, and the way he went about things might be less violent, but he was still the same person.

"Are you planning on returning to Odentia soon?" Kaia asked. Her voice was carefully controlled and diplomatic.

Rowena nodded. "We had planned to stay a little longer, but with all the events that have happened over these last few weeks, I want to get home. I want to make sure that Odentia moves in the path that is best for it, and I have a lot of work left to do, now more than ever."

"Understandable," Kaia nodded once.

Rowena looked first at Kaia, then at each of the others. "Thank you all for your help. I hope that we all might meet again soon without these clouds hanging over us."

"I hope so, too," Kaia said.

A knock came on the door, and Wickham twisted to see Hector step into the room. He wore the plain blue uniform that all students were given in their third year at the Institute. He nodded at the students. As Kaia stood, he hugged her.

"The carriage is ready," he said. "See you soon."

"Have a pleasant trip," Kaia said.

Hector turned to Rowena and offered her his hand. Her cheeks colored as she took it and stood. Wickham noted the way her fingers wrapped tightly around those of her husband. Perhaps there was genuine affection between them after all.

He hoped there was. He hated the idea that a marriage could be done only for political purposes. He couldn't understand how that sort of marriage could survive. How would they have children if they didn't love each other? It just seemed so... soulless otherwise.

But Kaia was right. They had chosen each other, and their reasons were their own. It wasn't up to him to judge the rightness of their marriage.

"What will you all be doing now?" Hector asked once Rowena stood beside him. His manner of speaking and the way he held himself was much more relaxed than hers.

"Head back to the Institute, I guess," Kaia replied. She glanced over her shoulder at the others.

Wickham nodded. "It's about time we return to our studies. With any luck, nothing else will go wrong this year."

"I hope so," Herja said with a sigh. "It's already difficult enough to study for our exams and the entrance exams for universities. The last thing we need is for it all to get even more difficult."

Rowena laughed musically. "I hope it works out for you all, too. Perhaps the next time we see each other, we will look at an even brighter future with no more of these tensions to contend with."

Wickham smiled. That would be very nice.

But it would never be that easy.

CHAPTER
THIRTEEN

Several days after returning to the Institute, Wickham sat in a chair across from Professor Carmilla. Her long silver hair was loose around her. Behind her glasses, gray eyes skimmed over the pamphlet that she held in her hands. Wickham twisted his hands in his lap. All the students were getting these one-on-one meetings with the professors, but he couldn't help but be nervous.

"So, you've already had a semester here?" Carmilla asked, looking up from the pamphlet.

"Yeah. Yes," Wickham corrected himself.

Apparently, sitting in an office discussing his future was even more intimidating than facing down the possibility of war.

Carmilla hummed as she folded the pamphlet back up. "You've been pursuing a medical career for some time, haven't you?"

Wickham's head bobbed. "After I got home from the Silver Springs, I learned my father was very sick. I ended up working with our local herbalist, wanting to help more than I could at the time. I've wanted to be a medic ever since."

"But what sort of medic?" Carmilla asked. "Doctor, nurse, herbalist, something else?"

"Right now, I intend to be a doctor," Wickham replied. "I want to be a general practitioner with a focus on herb-magics to provide healing. I still want to learn some elements of surgery. Herja and I will probably end up moving around a lot for her education and research afterward, and I want general skills I can apply anywhere."

Carmilla took off her glasses and set them aside. "I have never had a year of students who have already thought through and planned their futures as thoroughly as this year."

Wickham scratched the back of his neck. "Is that a bad thing?"

"No. It just makes it a little trickier for me to know how to help you all."

"Maybe we just don't need help," Wickham murmured, shrugging one of his shoulders. Even though he'd narrowed down his career path more over the years, it had been clear to him since he was thirteen years old.

It was the same for Penelope and Herja in other ways, too. He'd also heard Adina, Nolen, Xena, and Lena all explain what they were going to do once they graduated.

"So, this isn't normal?" he asked, frowning.

"It's unusual for people your age to have such a firm grasp on life," Carmilla replied. "Saying it's 'not normal' implies that there's something wrong with you. I suspect it's more of a trauma response than anything else. You have all had to grow up fast."

Wickham sighed. "I'm tired of hearing that. I don't feel like I grew up fast at all."

Carmilla smiled at him.

Wick! Herja connected mind-to-mind with him. *Penelope collapsed —we need you.*

Wickham leaped to his feet.

"What are you doing?" Carmilla asked, startled.

Wickham explained as he grabbed his stuff. Carmilla got to her feet as well, her eyes shifting focus briefly.

"She's in the hospital wing," Carmilla said, no doubt having reached out to the other professors mind-to-mind. "There's nothing you can do right now."

"I can be there," Wickham argued.

Carmilla dipped her chin.

Wickham rushed to the hospital wing, his heart hammering. He bolted up the stairs, and as he did so, he heard Kaia and Nolen's voices from somewhere behind him. Good. He wasn't waiting for them, though.

Soon, he was in the medical wing. Herja waited for him at the entrance to the wing and quickly hugged him. "I don't know what happened. We were sparring, and then she just collapsed. Raven's in with her as she's being examined. We're supposed to wait out here."

Kaia and Nolen joined them. Herja repeated the same thing, adding to the detail that Penelope had said something about feeling hungry just before she collapsed.

"Maybe it's just that she needed to eat," Kaia said as she twisted her hands.

A few minutes later, the nurse opened the door. She was wearing a mask and gloves as she ushered the four of them in. "Please come with me."

Wickham followed at the front of the group. He veered toward where he saw a single bed with the curtains pulled around it, but the nurse cleared her throat and shook his head. He hesitated, then stepped back in line.

They went into the nurse's office, where she showed all of them to wash their hands and put on masks of their own. Wickham did so and then slid the soft cloth over his nose and mouth. This had to be bad.

"Have you all had close contact with Penelope over the last few days?" the nurse asked.

Wickham nodded, as did the others.

"I'm afraid I'm going to have to put you all in isolation, then. Penelope is running a high fever; we aren't sure what it is, but when a dragon gets sick, it's usually highly contagious. You'll be quarantined for a few days, at least until we can figure out what's making her sick."

A chill ran down Wickham's spine. He opened his mouth, then shut it again.

Dragons didn't get sick. Their immune systems were too powerful to deal with most illnesses. For Penelope to develop a fever so suddenly was more than concerning—it was downright frightening. He looked at the others, who were all looking back at him; he was the one with medical knowledge, after all.

"Will we be quarantined together or separately?" he asked.

"Separately," the nurse replied, then handed them each a piece of paper. "Here's a list of symptoms for you all to look out for. If you feel any of these, inform the staff immediately. It doesn't matter how busy they are or at what time of night it is. If you're uncertain at all, inform them. This is a very serious matter."

Wickham glanced over the list: headache, sore throat, nausea, weakness, dizziness, feeling disoriented. There were more, too, and he breathed out a silent sigh. He couldn't think of any illnesses that had this many symptoms. Were they just casting a wide net?

This wasn't good, whatever it was. Where could Penelope have even gotten sick from?

An image of her in that swirling, sparkling mist within the gorgon mirror appeared in his head. And it only made his stomach squeeze tighter. Were they facing the next step of the sorcerer's plan?

∗∗∗

Herja cupped her chin in her hand, using the index finger of her other hand to follow along with the words she was trying to read.

The four of them were in a neat little row. Each of their beds was encased with walls of shimmering light; the quarantine. It would kill any airborne germs. Each small room had a bed, curtains, a self-cleaning chamber pot, and a desk with personal items ordered by the headmasters.

They'd been in here for a full day now. They were not to connect mind-to-mind to anyone, as this could be a magical disease spread through that contact.

Raven was within the quarantine space set up around Penelope. They refused to leave their mate alone and even now sat by her side, combing their fingers through Pen's fire-red hair. Raven had covered Penelope with the blanket they had woven with the star threads that bound them together.

Herja fingered the bracelet of her own star threads that matched Wickham's. He was reading through a book the doctors had given him about various dragon-specific diseases. His space was between her and Penelope, and he always had questions for the medics when they came around to check on Penelope.

"What are you reading?" Nolen asked from behind her. His quarantine space was between her and Kaia.

Herja turned. Nolen was the one who seemed to struggle most with quarantine. Herja understood; he was a very active dragon, and having no space to do more than tight pacing had to be driving him crazy.

"I'm studying," she told him.

"But all our exams are physical tests to show our skills," Nolen said, frowning. "So, what are you studying for?"

"For after we graduate from the Institute. I intend to get into the education sphere, and to do that; I'm going to need to get into a college or university. So I need to sit their entrance exams." Herja stood from her desk and stretched. She'd been sitting in a hunched position too long.

Nolen grunted in response, then sat on the edge of his bed. "Adina plans on getting into education, too."

"Different areas, though," Herja replied. "She's gonna be doing that early childhood stuff, and I intend on doing more research to help kids who might be slipping through our current system without the help they need."

"Ah. Yeah, I remember Kaia telling me about that now."

Nolen must be bored for him to continue talking to her like this. He was sociable when he needed to be, but he liked to stay in the background, which was just fine with Herja. Existing quietly in the same space together was just fine with her.

"Where are you going to apply to?" Nolen asked her.

"I haven't fully decided that yet. There are a few options, but I want to be somewhere that I can see Wickham often, even if we're not in the same city. I have four options that I'll be applying to over the summer."

Nolen nodded. "Kaia and I are planning to work with the Crown in an official ambassadorial position. Or at least Kaia will be the ambassador, and I'll be there to support her. Rowena and Lyra have both invited her to return to their respective kingdoms."

Herja nodded. Talking about their futures while Penelope was so sick seemed somehow wrong, but Herja couldn't think of anything else to discuss. She hadn't been exactly successful in her attempts to study, either.

The possibilities for her seemed far more open than they had a few years ago. Even now, she doubted herself. She had always thought she needed to be the very best if she wanted to be successful. If she wasn't the best, then she wasn't doing her best. Funnily enough, she hadn't put that same sort of pressure on other people.

With a sigh, she smoothed her black hair behind her ear. "You and Kaia will do good with that. You've already done so much to help with international relationships. But is it going to be okay for you? I know you run out of social energy quickly, too. Much quicker than Kaia."

Nolen shrugged. "Yeah, I do. But it's not as difficult as I thought it would be. I can keep to the back, and Kaia takes care of the major problems. There's always something for me to work on or fix. Build a fence while she talks to the farmers sort of thing."

"That sounds good."

Nolen smiled and glanced over his shoulder at Kaia. She was resting on her bed; her head pillowed on her arms. "We complement each other in that way. It works out well for the both of us."

Herja nodded as Nolen wandered away from the wall between them. She returned to her desk but found she couldn't concentrate on it.

Instead, she watched as Wickham read through his book. They were matched well, too. Both could get obsessive in whatever they were doing, but on the flip side, they easily found ways to fit it together. They had spent so much time in tranquil togetherness studying.

Herja smiled at her mate, her heartwarming at the sight of him. Penelope was going to get better, and with any luck, this was just going to be a late effect of the stress she had been other. Then she and Wickham could concentrate on their future together.

Everything was going to be okay. She didn't know how she'd handle it if it weren't.

CHAPTER

FOURTEEN

Frantic murmurs woke Kaia in the middle of the night. She burrowed deeper into her blankets, trying to ignore them, until she heard Penelope's name. Her eyes shot wide open as adrenaline coursed through her. With her heart in her throat, she threw back her blankets and jumped out of bed. The hooks holding the curtain screeched as she yanked them aside.

The quarantine barriers were still up, but light spilled into the medical bay from Penelope's space. Nurses and doctors moved through the barrier, all wearing fully protective gear.

"What's going on?" she demanded, not bothering to keep her voice down.

Nolen drew his curtains back. Either he had gone to sleep in his uniform, or he'd changed before checking.

The medical personnel ignored her question, continuing to bustle around Penelope's bed.

"Hello?" Kaia called out, pressing both her hands against the quarantine barrier. "Can someone please tell me what's happened? Is Penelope okay?"

Herja and Wickham both emerged from their curtains, too. They watched the personnel for a moment, then Herja hurried around her bed to be closer to Nolen.

"Have either of you seen anything?"

Kaia shook her head. Her stomach churned. Had something terrible happened? Was that why the medics refused to tell them anything?

"Raven?" she called. If someone knew what was happening, it would be them, right?

Her heart jumped to her throat as Penelope's voice rang out, high and clear. "For goodness sake! They're going to be freaking out; someone has to tell them something."

The curtains around Penelope's bed drew back. The red of her hair glowed in the dim light stone flicker. Kaia couldn't see her face clearly, but she held herself up as though she hadn't even been sick. Raven sat in the chair next to the bed, hands gripping the armrests tightly.

"I'm fine," Penelope called, but there was something overly cheerful in her voice. "The fever broke. So you can all go back to sleep. I'm sorry that I've caused such a hullabaloo."

Kaia's knees went weak with relief. She stumbled back to her bed and sagged into it, staring past the rest of them toward Penelope. Wickham rounded his own bed to be close to the barrier separating his bed from Penelope's, but Penelope stepped back.

"I don't think it's a good idea to ask questions," she blurted. "Not yet, at least. Let the doctors figure out what happened. But you should all go back to bed now."

Wickham started talking in a low voice, but exhaustion rushed over Kaia. She hadn't slept for the past two days and had barely gotten any rest during the day, despite not having much to do. Her stomach was tied up into too many knots, worried about Penelope.

Now, though, Penelope was okay. Her fever had broken, which meant she would soon recover. That meant she could finally relax enough to sleep. Her shoulders slumped, too tired to hold them straight anymore. She drew the curtains around her bed and rolled herself back into the blankets.

Penelope was okay.

The worst was over.

From here on out, everything was going to be okay.

Penelope was okay.

When Kaia opened her eyes to the sunlight streaming into the room the next morning, it was the only thought in her head. Penelope was okay, which meant they would all be released from quarantine and get back to normal life.

As she lay in her bed, staring up at the ceiling, a sudden fear struck her. What if she had just dreamed the whole thing last night?

Quickly, she detangled herself from her blankets and threw on a dressing gown, then yanked back the curtains. Just like the previous night, they squealed when she did so. Unlike the night, though, the glittering quarantine barrier was gone. Her breath caught in her throat as she cautiously stepped forward.

But it wasn't just her eyes playing tricks on her. The barrier was gone. Relief broke out through her as she rushed past the other three beds, still with their curtains around them, to Penelope's bed.

Penelope sat in the bed, with Raven sitting over the blankets on one side and Headmaster Valiant sitting in the chair. Kaia came up short, but Headmaster Valiant gave her a welcoming nod.

Kaia rushed forward and threw her arms around Penelope. "You're okay! I was so worried. It must just have been stress. But you're okay—"

She froze as she pulled back.

Penelope stared at her, a grim, expectant look on her face. Her eyes were locked on Kaia's, but as hard as Kaia tried to control her expression, she could feel all her emotions pouring over her face. All the while, Penelope's eyes stared at her.

Her blue eyes.

Not silver. Not the color of a dragon's eyes. Blue, as they had been before, she drank from the Silver Springs.

Kaia's arms dropped to her sides. She opened her mouth, but nothing came out. What was she supposed to say?

"I can't connect to her mind-to-mind," Raven said. Their voice was ragged like they had been crying.

Kaia turned to Headmaster Valiant. "What happened? This isn't possible!"

"Shhh," Penelope said, flapping her hands at Kaia. "Don't wake the others."

Kaia pressed her lips together, trying to hold in any further exclamations of surprise. She desperately wanted to ask what happened but was afraid if she spoke, it'd come out as a shriek.

"I know you must be very stressed and afraid," Headmaster Valiant said. "But whatever happened to Penelope is only affecting other dragons. You don't have to worry about yourself."

Other dragons? Kaia's throat went dry as she looked back at the line of beds with the surrounding curtains. Far more were occupied now than they were when she had woken up last night. From this spot, she saw Wickham's bed was empty, but she saw his shoes under the curtain next to Herja's bed.

"Headmaster Twila has come down with the illness as well," Headmaster Valiant said. His voice was so carefully controlled it made Kaia feel even more sick to her stomach. "However, we have been receiving reports from all over Eldavon. It started with the dragons who were at the wedding and have quickly spread from there."

Kaia turned on her heel. Blood rushed in her ears as she strode down the line to Herja's bed. She hesitated a moment, then opened the curtain. Herja jerked and looked up. She lay in the bed, her arms wrapped around herself while Wickham sat next to her, smoothing her hair down.

Fever flushed Herja's cheeks a bright red. Was it just Kaia's imagination that her eyes looked duller?

"Kaia," Wickham said in surprise. "What are you—"

She moved past them and slipped into the curtains surrounding Nolen's bed. He was asleep still, sweat dotting his forehead. When Kaia moved forward and touched his skin, she found it as hot as if he was in a furnace. Her stomach roiled as she closed her eyes and sank into the chair.

It started with the people at the wedding, which meant King Lantos... and Hector. They would be sick, too. Her father. Countless others. What was going on? What did this mean? Would the dragon be burned out of all of them with this fever?

She shook as the possibilities welled up in her mind. All she could think was this was some sort of trick, some sort of trap.

Had Finnegan done something when he drank from the Springs? Had he poisoned it somehow to make the dragons lose their magic? Had he used it to mix up some sort of spell that he used to put on the dragons at the wedding?

He was the easiest target for the blame, but somehow Kaia didn't think that was even possible. He'd been so genuinely concerned with Rowena. He'd seemed to be steadfast in his desire for them to avoid a war. The apology he had given her, Adina, and Icarus just felt too real.

Which left the sorcerer.

Kaia's hands tightened as she gazed down at her mate. Nolen was her perfect match. Her protector. The one she relied on more than anyone else. To see him suffering like this made anger well up in her; she hadn't known she was capable of.

He might not lose his dragon. We don't know what this is. We don't know what's happening.

But she didn't need time to tell her what would happen. No. What she needed was to figure out how to find the sorcerer and what magic they were using to do this.

And then stop them.

⁂

The days that followed were a blur of anxiety, fear, and relentless work. Wickham was constantly busy, all the while with worry eating at him. He wanted first to stay at Herja's bedside and then to leave her, only to take care of Rhett when his brother fell ill, too. The medical bay became a constant flurry of activity.

"I wanted to be taken seriously as a medic, but not because of a situation like this," he told Kaia three days later, stretching his aching back. He'd been on his feet for almost twelve hours helping in the medical wing.

Kaia pushed his bowl of stew closer to him. "Eat. You're going to collapse, and then you won't be able to help."

Wickham sighed, knowing she was right. He'd been brought into the medical wing as an honorary nurse. He was giving the sick dragons medications, food, water, cleaning up after them, and everything that the fully trained staff did as well.

They had help on the way, but with no dragons to fly them to the Institute, they would wait for some time for their backup to arrive.

He ate one bite of the stew, finding it lukewarm and not delicious. His stomach rumbled, gratefully accepting anything he would give it.

"Have you found out anything about the mirrors and the Sorcerer?" Wickham asked between bites of food.

Kaia shook her head. "I've been reading through all of Herja's books, but I'm just not as fast as she is. I can't tell if anything I'm finding is actually useful."

Wickham rubbed his prickling, dry eyes. He'd been going so hard all day that he hadn't realized how tired he actually was. Now that he was sitting and had a half-bowl of food in his stomach, he felt as though he could lie down on the floor and pass out right there.

"Nolen's fever went away this morning," Kaia said as she rested her head in her hands. "His eyes aren't silver anymore."

Wickham winced. Herja was still sleeping, but her fever had drastically reduced, too. He knew in the pit of his stomach that when she woke, she wouldn't have her dragon anymore, either. It made him feel sick. He almost wished he'd burst into the same sort of fever, so he could at least lose his magic with her.

It wasn't logical, and he knew it would just end up being worse for Herja, too, if such a thing happened. He couldn't help it, though.

"I can't help but think this was what the sorcerer was after from the start," Kaia said, her eyes glazed—she hadn't been sleeping, either. "Without the dragons to protect us, Eldavon is vulnerable. How will we protect ourselves now? And what will the other kingdoms do once they find out?"

Wickham closed his eyes. These were questions he had been deliberately fighting against thinking. If he started down that path, he'd end up spiraling into despair.

"Odentia is our ally now," he nodded. "And we have other kingdoms that are friends. It's going to be okay."

"You're right."

The sound of Kaia's chair scraping against the floor made Wickham look up again. Her expression had transformed, and she threw her shoulders back, glaring at the wall now.

"Odentia is our ally, and Hector is my cousin. This started with Rowena and the gorgon mirrors. So it's going to end with the gorgon mirrors." She nodded once as though that settled it. "How long until the additional medics get here?"

"They should arrive in a couple of days."

"All right. Then in the meantime, I'll talk with Headmaster Valiant," Kaia said, her gaze moving back to Wickham. "We're going to Odentia."

CHAPTER
FIFTEEN

Penelope had grown so used to seeing silver eyes staring back at her she no longer recognized her own face in the mirror. She still felt like herself, as though if she just reached out, she'd find her dragon form and be able to slip into that form as easily as taking a breath. But it wasn't there. No matter how hard she searched, no matter what she did to bring it back, it wasn't there.

She wasn't the only one who had lost their dragon. Nolen and Herja were both awake now, the silver leeched from their eyes. Headmaster Valiant, Row, and all the professors. Half the dragon students were still in fever, but the other half had recovered already.

Can anyone hear me? She thought, trying hard to project it out of herself. But only silence answered her.

"All right. So I need to stop doing that because it only makes me feel worse," she said aloud.

She turned from the mirror. With a dragon or without, she was still Penelope. Was she still her... right? Even though it felt as though she was missing half of who she was.

Her clothes lay over her bed, with her backpack sitting on her pillow. Kaia had made all the arrangements for them to connect the mirror portal they had here to the one in Odentia. The gorgon mirrors had arrived from the palace late last night, carried by relay runners who had protected the delicate artifacts.

Part of Penelope wondered if things were even worse than she thought since the Crown was relying on the six students once more. She knew they must be working on their own solutions, but it just felt off for Kaia to have gotten permission for this plan of hers so quickly.

A knock came on the door, making her jump.

Penelope shoved her clothes into the pack, not bothering to check exactly what she had. When she came to her blue uniform, she shoved it under her pillow so she wouldn't have to look at it.

"Penelope?" Raven asked.

Penelope winced and looked over her shoulder. Raven was wearing all gray, reminding her of the ancient gorgon spirits they had met on their adventures over the summer.

"Is everyone else ready to go?" Penelope asked.

"Nolen and Kaia told me to let you know we're going to be delayed for about half an hour. They're talking to the headmasters right now." Raven gently took the pack from her and pulled her clothes back out. "So we have time to fold these properly."

Penelope sighed heavily. "Do you really think that I should come along on this? I feel like I will not do much good."

"We need you," Raven replied.

"But why?"

Raven folded her clothes. "Because you are our friend and a vital part of our group. You've always been part of it. You, Herja, Kaia, and Wickham are the core. Nolen and I are part of it now, yeah, but we still rely on the rest of you. And you are a hub in the wheel of our crossroads. We won't get anything done without you."

Penelope couldn't help but smile at that. It sounded rather poetic. She supposed that was the purpose.

Quietly, she layered her shirts together and rolled them to maximize the space in her pack. She wasn't sure how long they would end up being in Odentia.

"It's going to work out," Raven murmured, reaching out to run their fingers up and down Penelope's spine.

The contact felt good and helped to relax some of Penelope's tension. "How can you be sure that it's going to work out, though?"

"Last night, I dreamed about the stars throwing a drop spindle between each other, but they weren't creating new threads. They were strengthening ones they had already made."

Penelope nodded. She wasn't entirely certain that meant anything at all... but if she still had her dragon, she would have trusted Raven. There was no reason not to trust them now.

Once she was done packing, Penelope shouldered her pack and helped Raven put on their backpack; then, they headed to the portal mirror. Herja and Wickham were already waiting with Row.

"Are you sure you have everything?" Row asked, their eyes on Herja and a crinkle in their brow.

Penelope couldn't look at their face; they just didn't look the same without their silver eyes.

"I'm sure," Herja said, lifting her bookbag. "Enough food and water to last us a few days, a self-cleaning chamber pot, and all the books I need to continue my research."

"We don't need all of that," Raven protested.

Wickham, carrying a satchel, shook his head. "And I don't need to bring along as much medical supplies. Being over-prepared is making me feel better. Herja packed all that on my request."

Raven dipped their head toward Wickham.

Shortly after, Kaia and Nolen joined them, along with Headmasters Valiant and Twila. Twila leaned heavily on a cane, looking exceedingly small and frail.

"Are you ready?" Valiant asked them all.

Row stepped back, their face more worried than ever. It made Penelope nervous; Row was usually so stoic.

She reached out and took Raven's hand, bolstering herself. "We're ready."

"We haven't been able to contact anyone in Odentia via mind-to-mind," Valiant warned. "We don't know what you're going to find."

"We're ready," Penelope repeated.

Valiant studied her, then nodded. He stepped through the students and laid his fingers against the cool obsidian. It took a moment, but the black, dull face rippled after a moment, showing the view of a gray stone wall. A window in the wall showed a dark sky with fat flakes of snow floating past the glass.

Penelope breathed out a deep breath. There had been so much happening it hadn't even occurred to her how strange it was that they didn't have snow on the ground here at the Institute.

Valiant stepped back, and Penelope tightened her grip on Raven's hand. Well. Here went nothing. She strode forward, Raven beside her, and stepped through the mirror.

The transition was as smooth as stepping through a doorway. As she moved out of the way of the others, she shivered—it was far colder here than it had been at Eldavon! Looking around, she found they had stepped through to a plain stone room. The mirror was propped up in the middle of it.

"We thought you might be coming."

Penelope turned. Rowena and Hector stood in the doorway, holding hands.

"You've lost your dragon, too," she said, meeting Hector's dark eyes.

"And so have you," he said, his shoulders slumping. "Follow us. There's a lot we need to talk about."

Herja followed at the back of the group, fighting to get herself back under control. She wasn't sure why seeing Hector and Rowena made this complete disaster suddenly feel very real to her. Now her hands shook, and she wasn't sure what she was supposed to do about it.

The same way I dealt with disappointments in the past, she told herself. *I didn't get strong when I was revealed as a dragon. I've always been strong, and with my friends, I'm even stronger.*

She quickly brushed away the tears burning her eyes and inhaled deeply. She would not end up in a mess on the floor. There was no point in falling apart.

They entered a parlor decorated in pastel blues and greens. A fire roared in a marble hearth, warming the space up against the storm, which blew harder outside. There were two sets of doors here, one which led back to the portal mirror and one on the opposite side of the room, which presumably led to the rest of the Odentian palace.

Rowena headed to the opposite door and locked it.

"This has to be the sorcerer's work," Herja said, unable to stand the silence any longer. "We brought the gorgon mirrors with us. I figure we can look for other artifacts, and, in the meantime, we wanted to apprise you of what was going on, so you can be prepared."

Hector nodded. "We believe it's the sorcerer as well. If he wants to start wars, then taking away Eldavon's army is the best way to do it."

"So the first thing we need to do is to figure out if we can use the mirrors to get through to wherever the sorcerer is," Herja said.

"No," Rowena said softly. "That's not the first thing we should do at all. First, we have a lot of information to discuss and convey to each other. The witches here at the palace could not reach back to Eldavon and contact the Crown. Do you have any way of taking information back to them?"

Penelope gestured back the way they came. "The mirror."

Hector shook his head. "We've been trying to activate it without success."

They should have seen this coming. Herja bit her lips together to stop herself from exclaiming aloud. Of course, if the dragons at the wedding were first hit, Hector would have been as well. They should have thought more about a way to get information back to Eldavon.

Raven held out their hands to either side silently.

"Will it do any good?" Herja asked doubtfully. Wickham and Kaia joined hands, with Wickham also holding Raven's.

Raven turned their head toward her. "I've been able to connect with dragons, witches, humans, mermaids, krakens, rocs, and dead people. I'm pretty sure that you not having your dragon now will not make any difference."

Well. When they said it like that. Herja took Raven's free hand and offered her other hand to Nolen. Everyone linked up. Herja couldn't feel the connection, not like before, but after a few minutes, Kaia and Wickham both grinned.

"We can reach Adina, Lena, Icarus, and Jalene."

"Good." Rowena dropped her hands, breaking the circle. "Because there is something else which is just as trouble that we need to report... and I just pray this isn't my fault."

Surprise rippled through Herja. Why would she blame herself for any of this? Tension crept up her neck. What had the queen done? It couldn't be on purpose, not when her eyes were as worried as they were.

"What is it?" Penelope asked.

Rowena winced, then shook her head. "It will be better to show you."

She walked across the room to a set of long, heavy drapes. She pulled them aside to reveal yet another door, though this one was filled with panes of glass and led outside. Herja reached for Wickham's hand as they stepped into the falling snow.

The cold slapped Herja across the face. She breathed in a biting breath and moved closer to Wickham so they could share their warmth.

They were now standing in an open courtyard. Walls rose ten feet on every side, and the misshapen lumps under the snow spoke to various plants that must be beautiful in the summer. Herja's head turned this way, and as she looked for whatever it was, Rowena was trying to show them.

"There," Hector said, pointing to the sky.

Herja looked up and gasped. Cutting through the sky like a fiery sword was a dragon. It was as red as fire, the same color as Penelope's hair. It dove and spun with elegance. The play stopped suddenly, and the dragon circled above them, then descended; it appeared it didn't quite know how to do this, going into a dive before coming up sharply and circling again.

"I don't understand," Kaia said. "That almost looks like your dragon."

"It looks exactly like my dragon," Hector replied grimly. "Not just the color and the size. It has the same armored scales along its back and belly, the same proto-horns on its head. And even more. The scars along my wings that I got when I foolishly picked a fight with a bear."

Herja inhaled deeply as the dragon finally came to land before them. Her heart beat so shallowly she almost couldn't feel it.

The dragon retook their natural form, and this horrible feeling choking her grew even worse. Finnegan's eyes glowed silver, and though he attempted to put on a grave expression, he still grinned.

So they had been right from the start...

Finnegan really was behind everything.

CHAPTER
SIXTEEN

Wickham felt the hostility rolling off Herja as she rolled to the balls of her feet.

Anxiety spiked through him. Yes, she had been trained in hand-to-hand combat in her natural form and her dragon form. But that didn't mean she was used to fighting against someone like Finnegan, and besides that, he was a dragon now. He could take Hector's stolen dragon form and then...

Wickham wrapped his arms around Herja's waist, trying to remind her they couldn't afford to anger Finnegan now. His heart slammed into his ribs, and his gaze quickly darted to Rowena. Did she know what was going on? Was she in on Finnegan's plot?

"This is what we need to report to Eldavon," the young queen said, gesturing at her uncle. "He woke up just this morning with the ability to do this, and we don't know why?"

"Don't you?" Penelope asked. It sounded like an accusation.

Finnegan ruffled his hair as he looked at them. To Wickham's surprise, he didn't pull out that arrogant expression he'd used so often in their previous conflicts.

"I'm just as confused about all of this as you are," Finnegan told them. "This isn't something I did on purpose, no matter what you think."

"And why would you assume we'd think that unless you did it on purpose?" Nolen demanded.

Wickham sighed—that was actually quite an obvious answer. "It would be more strange if we didn't assume he was behind it. Of course, he'd be the one we accused out of instinct."

Nolen glanced over at him and scowled. But he inclined his head. He'd put Kaia on his other side, toward the center of their group. Wickham couldn't blame him.

"Wick?" Herja murmured. "I need you to let me go."

Reluctantly, Wickham dropped his arms. He just had to trust that she would do nothing foolish—which, as he thought about it, was highly unlikely. Herja was too smart to make an impulsive decision that would harm them all.

"You're happy about this, though," Wickham said to Finnegan. "You can't deny it. You're thrilled to have Hector's dragon form."

"I'm thrilled to have a dragon form and to fly," Finnegan corrected, a shadow crossing his face. "I'm not happy that I have the form that belongs to Hector. But regardless, this has happened, and we should figure out why."

Penelope lifted her hand. "Yes, we should. But we are exposed out here. We should go back indoors so we can have a better discussion."

Finnegan nodded his head toward her, and Rowena led back into her parlor. Wickham sighed as the warmth of the room washed over him; he hadn't even realized he was getting cold until now. Finnegan closed the drapes over the door after he came in, then took a spot standing behind Rowena as she took a seat on the couch, Hector beside her.

"So the first question is, is this because I drank from the Silver Springs at the wedding?" Finnegan asked.

"I doubt it," Herja said, shaking her head. She and Wickham shared a narrow chair; he sat on the seat while she perched on the armrest. "There isn't a limited amount of magic to go around, so it makes no sense that the Springs would take the dragon from one person to give it to another. I've never heard of anything like this before."

Wickham nodded his agreement. "Besides, it would have no effect on the other dragons throughout Eldavon. Which reminds me, we need to relay this information back to the Crown."

"Right," Raven said.

They held their hands out. Wickham took Herja's and reached over to Hector's. They all joined, and Raven bowed their head. After a few minutes, they nodded. "Eldavon thanks us for the information and will work on it as they can—they'd like us to check in every day so we can update each other."

Rowena nodded. "I'm glad to have it. Now, we have the witches Hazel and Henri here, along with the dragons Kiango and Saffron still. Although..."

"They're not dragons anymore," Wickham finished for her, grim-faced.

Rowena sighed but nodded again. "No. They fell ill for three days, and when they recovered, they no longer had their dragons."

"The witches still have their magic, though, correct?" Penelope asked.

"Yes."

"Good. We should collaborate as soon as possible."

Hector cleared his throat. "They are currently with their mates, but we'll inform them of your arrival as soon as we're finished up here. Now. You said something about artifacts?" he asked Herja.

"Yes. Since we know the Sorcerer used the gorgon mirrors, I believe he must have access to other artifacts that allowed him to do this. Any stories that Odentia has about this sort of thing or anything similar will help us."

"*They*," Raven whispered. "We can't assume that the sorcerer is a man. If we do, we're limiting ourselves, and it'll be less likely for us to find out who they really are if they're not a man."

Herja nodded at Raven. "Yes. Them."

Wickham twisted his hands. He wanted to go talk with Hazel and

Henri at once to see if they had any further information about this illness that he and the other medics had overlooked.

"The six of you will have access to everything you need," Rowena told them. "If anyone gives you trouble, tell me, Hector, or my uncle. We will resolve the problems for you. Under my orders, you are to be given anything you need."

"You still need to give that order," Finnegan told her gently.

Rowena sighed as she rubbed her temples. "Yes. Of course. I'll also have chambers made up for you. Do you all want separate rooms, or do any of you wish to share?"

"We'll take one room with the six of us," Penelope said.

Wickham fought not to grimace. All six of them in one room? He supposed it wasn't much different from having to share a tent. It seemed more uncomfortable to be indoors, though.

"All of you?" Rowena asked, her eyes widening.

Penelope nodded. "Six beds in one room, and it would be appreciated if we could have a few partisans so we can figure out how to we want to arrange for our own privacy."

"I'll arrange it," Hector said.

"Thank you," Rowena said. "This stress is making me feel a little tired and ill. Let's get this sorted, so I can go lie down."

Wickham dug into his medical pouch and found some nausea tablets. "Here. These will help your stomach."

Rowena took them, looking a little surprised. "Thank you. Now. Let's get this going, shall we?"

⁂

The room they were given was plenty big enough for all six of their beds. They organized the beds in two rows, with three in each row, headboards against the walls. They used partisans to create a small changing space. The hearth was in the primary space, which allowed them to stay warm throughout the night.

Kaia couldn't sleep. She lay still, not wanting to toss and turn and disturb the others. Her mind raced over everything that had been discussed throughout the day. She wasn't sure how she was supposed to deal with it all.

At some point, she heard a heavy sigh and the rustle of blankets. She carefully turned to see who it was. Nolen climbed out of his bed and pulled a dressing gown over his pajamas, then padded toward the door leading to the rest of the palace.

Kaia hesitated only a moment before she, too, slipped from her bed. She pulled on her dressing gown and shoved her feet into her slippers, and hurried out after him. The hallway was chilly, and she shivered, glad she had remembered her slippers. Nolen was walking down the hallway toward a window at the far end.

"Hey," Kaia called as she went after him, careful not to be too loud.

Nolen turned and waited for her. He held his hand to her, and they tiptoed to the window, staring out. It was a cloudless night, and the moon reflecting on the snow made it look bright and beautiful.

"Are you okay?" Kaia asked in a low voice.

"I don't think so."

Kaia leaned against his side in silent support.

"I just keep wondering what all of this means. Not just for Eldavon but for us. Can we still be fated mates when I'm not a dragon?"

Kaia winced, sucking in a deep breath. The pain in his words cut right through her. "Of course we are. I love you, and we're fated mates, no matter what."

"All our plans were hinging on me being a dragon, though."

"Then we'll change our plans," Kaia replied bracingly. "It doesn't matter to me what happens, just as long as we can be together. I have every confidence that we can figure this out, Nolen. You will get your dragon back."

Nolen turned to her, his eyes filled with worry. "And if I don't?"

Kaia brushed her fingers against his cheek. "We'll figure it out."

She meant every word, but he seemed dissatisfied with her answer, somehow. Kaia wished she could reassure him. She wanted him to realize that even if things were to change, that didn't mean the core of what they were together had to change.

"I love you," she repeated.

"I love you, too. I just... I just worry about everything. And whether I can protect you still."

"Your protective streak didn't start when you became a dragon, and it won't end now," Kaia teased lightly. "We'll get through this. I promise you."

Nolen smiled at her, stroking her silver curls back from her face. "Thanks. And I'm sorry for waking you up. I was trying to be quiet."

"I wasn't sleeping."

They stood there together, watching the world outside. Nerves squeezed Kaia's stomach, but she tried to push it aside. They would see this through. They'd figure out what they needed to do for the future.

Eventually, they turned back to leave—but even as they did so, a dark form caught Kaia's eyes. She pressed her hands to the glass, peering closer.

A dragon flipped through the air. At first, she thought it was Finnegan again. But as the dragon came closer to the palace, she saw it was turquoise—Penelope's dragon. She flew down and landed in the courtyard, then shifted—

Kaia gasped.

It was Rowena.

Rowena was a dragon now... holding Penelope's dragon form. She turned to Nolen, who looked just as alarmed as she did.

Whatever was happening... it was spreading.

CHAPTER
SEVENTEEN

Herja folded her arms, watching Rowena observe her own eyes in the mirror.

"What happened to me?" Rowena asked. Though her voice was flat and exhausted, at the end of her question, her breathing hitched. She lowered the mirror and turned to them all.

Kaia and Nolen had told them all what they had seen just before Hector came to their room, asking them to come to Rowena's parlor. Hazel, Kiango, Saffron, and Henri were there, too, but they looked just as lost as the rest of them.

"It looks as though whatever is happening, it's transferring our dragons to others," Kiango said, his arms tight across his chest.

"But why?" Rowena demanded. "And how do we stop it? I don't like this. I want my eyes back."

Herja dropped her arms; just looking at Kiango made her more tense when she noted the clear signs that he was angry. Maybe if she softened her stance, it would do a little to help ease the tension that flickered between them all like lightning.

Of course, it didn't help that everyone kept shooting Finnegan uncertain, even accusing, glances.

"Whatever is causing this must have started with you and Penelope in the gorgon mirrors," Herja said. "Illnesses can be spread by a person before they even know they're sick. I suspect that when Finnegan drank from the Springs, it triggered the switch to happen before yours."

Rowena rubbed her forehead. "All right. But how do we reverse it?"

Herja shook her head helplessly and glanced at the others. Everyone looked just as confused and helpless as she felt. Frustration welled in her, but she breathed deeply, trying to dispel it. They just needed time. They needed to read through the books and search out any artifacts that might have done this.

The door to the parlor opened, and one of the Odentia guards wandered in.

"What are you doing?" Finnegan snapped at him. "Get back to you—"

"Presenting the Sorcerer Silas to Queen Rowena," the guard said. His voice was flat and monotone, his eyes glassy.

Herja jumped to her feet. The Sorcerer?

"He comes to give his aid and gifts to the young queen of Odentia," the guard continued as though he couldn't hear the murmurs that burst out through the room. "Sacred are the Sorcerer's arts."

The guard stepped aside and bowed toward the door. Herja moved closer to Wickham, her hands clenched. A man swept into the room, strutting with his chest puffed out, and chin raised high.

He was dressed in opulent, pompous golden armor that glimmered with every movement. It was engraved with images of dragons, flowers, and geometric designs that almost looked like runes. A plumed hat rested atop his head; it was scarlet and also embroidered in the same geometric designs. The feathers were shades of blue, purple, and red.

He grinned as his bright eyes passed over everyone in the room, as though he was making sure that everyone was looking at him.

Once he was assured that he had the attention he was looking for, he bowed deeply to Rowena, sweeping off his enormous hat as he did so. The feathers brushed against the floor. His hair was a bland blond color, and he had a balding patch right at the crown of his head.

"Greetings, my queen," he said as he straightened and fixed his hat back on his head. "I heard your prayers for aid and have traveled from beyond the sea, sensing great distress in the land. I am here to rescue your kingdom from those that would cause it harm."

Herja made a disgusted noise in her throat while several of the others choked on disbelief. She couldn't make herself speak, though; she was still reeling from the sorcerer revealing himself so easily. Did he not know that they had already figured out his game?

"To my aid?" Rowena asked. Her skirts swished against the floor. "Forgive me, but I seem to recall your voice—you stole me from my tent and kept me in a space of cold sleep with no escape."

The sorcerer put a hand on his chest and bowed his head. "A mistake made by those I sent to protect you. I foresaw in a dream that villains this side of the sea meant to destroy you. You have a grand purpose to restore the balance of magic in this world—I could not allow that to happen."

He lifted his head once more. Herja opened her mouth, then closed it again. So he knew about the unbalanced magic? Did that mean he was trying to correct it and that he had nothing to do with it becoming unbalanced in the first place?

Silas smiled at Rowena, then turned his attention back to the others. "And what is this? Did Eldavon send a bunch of children to rope you into following their will? I have never seen a sadder bunch of witches—but no matter. Eldavon is built on its own self-righteousness, and perhaps children will see the fog they have put in your minds."

Kiango shifted slightly so he was standing in front of Hazel. "You are the one who has started all of this. Undo it. Give us our dragons back."

"If Eldavon was worthy of dragons, they never would have lost them in the first place," Silas replied with a shrug.

"And what's that supposed to mean?" Herja asked loudly, over the protests of the others. She balled her fists onto her hips as she glared at Silas. "What did we do that made us unworthy?"

"A child cannot understand when they are as overwrought with emotions as you are. Besides, I don't answer to little girls without magic," he said.

Herja snarled under her breath.

Rowena tossed her hair. "You will answer to me, though. Now answer the question, Silas. What are your plans here? Why have you come, and what do you want?"

Silas looked startled for a moment like he couldn't quite believe that Rowena was speaking to him in such a tone. He licked his lips, glanced around again, then smiled, seemingly to placate the queen.

"Which is most important, your Majesty? Which question would you like answered first?"

Herja nudged Wickham toward the others as Rowena answered. "Why do you say Eldavon lost their dragons because of unworthiness? Do you deny you had a hand in it?"

"Denying? No. No, I used the ancient rites to move magic," Silas replied. "As did the first dragon-witch king and queen did long ago, when they took magic from beyond the sea and placed it in Mount Eldavon. It's an ancient spell that allows the Earth to move magic about to the place where the worthiest dwell."

Herja squinted at him. "That doesn't sound like anything I've heard before."

"Knowledge that was deliberately kept from you," Silas said with that same arrogant tone he'd used with her before.

"And why are you here?" Rowena asked. "What do you want from Odentia?"

Silas removed his hat once again, rearranging his expression. "Ah, I intend to continue the work I have already started. Eldavon has hoarded magic too long. I intend to stand at your side as an advisor as you use the gifts the earth has given you to redistribute magic to all kingdoms under your banner."

"You mean you want Rowena to conquer the other kingdoms?" Kaia demanded.

"Yes."

"That's not good! You can't—"

"It is the only way to balance magic once more. Once the balance of magic is restored, these droughts that plague the other kingdoms will end; why do you think it has not touched Odentia?" His gaze focused on Rowena again. "Because you are meant to rule over them all."

Herja's mouth went dry as Rowena's expression became thoughtful. Then she smiled, and Herja's heart dropped to her stomach.

She was buying into this. No matter what she'd said about wanting her own eyes back... she was going to do exactly what Silas wanted.

<hr />

Kaia pressed her fingertips to her forehead, trying to make sense of it all. If Eldavon was supposed to have been allowing others to drink from the Silver Springs, wouldn't it have been better to explain this to the Crown? Instead of moving magic to another kingdom and causing violence, why not open up the Springs to all?

"You're talking as though war is a good thing," Kiango spat, echoing Kaia's thoughts. "It's evil to start such violence for personal gain. You can't be—"

"Personal gain?" Silas arched a brow at him. "No, no. For the good of all the kingdoms."

"But—" Kaia started.

Finnegan cleared his throat loudly, striding forward to stand next to Rowena. He cast an arrogant look over the Eldavon people. "Niece, we should not continue this discussion in front of these people. They will only keep arguing about their own kingdom's exceptionalism. We should talk with the sorcerer alone."

Kaia shook her head. "Rowena, I—"

"Queen." Rowena turned to her. "I am a queen, Kaia. Queen Rowena or Your Majesty. Do you understand?"

Kaia was too stunned to answer.

"My uncle is quite right. I am the queen here," she said, drawing herself up as she looked over all of them. "I have to think of what is best for my kingdom. You have all served Eldavon's purposes. I cannot have you questioning everything that Silas says, preventing me from seeing his side of this situation."

Kaia glanced at Kiango, Saffron, and the two witches. The four of them looked stunned and angry, but Hazel bowed toward Rowena.

"Of course, your Majesty. We will return to our chambers." There was an edge to her voice...

And Kaia realized it was because they wouldn't be allowed to return to their chambers at all. If Rowena really intended to turn on Eldavon, she would make sure that they couldn't escape and warn the Crown.

Which meant they had to do that right away. Not the escape part, but the warning part.

"We will go, too," she blurted. Then, remembering herself, she curt-sied deeply. "If Your Majesty will permit us."

Silas smiled at her. "Clever little girl."

Bile rose in her throat. She hated the way he was looking at her. She tried to ignore it, though, as she turned to her classmates. Nolen looked furious as he opened his mouth, but she put her hand over his lips and shook her head.

"We need to get back to our chambers," she whispered.

Penelope and Herja glanced at each other, then Herja led the way after Kiango and the others, with Penelope taking up a spot behind them. As they passed Hector, Kaia reached out to pull him with them —he had to know what their plans were.

He pulled his hand away from her, glaring at Silas. "I am her Majesty's husband, the Prince Consort. I have a right to be here, too."

Kaia slowed, but Wickham touched her shoulder, encouraging her to continue. She looked back helplessly as her cousin stood next to Rowena, his shoulders stiff as he stared at Silas. But it was Finnegan who worried her, given the smirk he had on his face.

"One moment," he said, causing the Eldavon procession to stop.

Finnegan bent to Rowena's ear, and she nodded.

"Guards," she called.

The two that stood outside her parlor straightened.

"Kiango, Hazel, Saffron, and Henri are to be escorted to their respective chambers and not allowed to leave or receive visitors. And as for these six," she gestured to the students, "they may be kept in the same room but move their beds further apart and shackle one hand to the headboard. Lightly—I do not wish for them to be harmed."

"You must be kidding," Penelope breathed.

"I don't want you to tell any wild stories to Eldavon's crown. Make sure they don't touch each other as you escort them to their chambers."

And that was it, was it? Kaia dropped her chin to her chest, heart aching. That was that, then. They couldn't warn Eldavon after all. So what were they going to do now?

EIGHTEEN

Penelope glared at the heavy shackle on her wrist. It was tight, but thanks to the leather cuff that the guards had put around her wrist first, she didn't think she was being bruised. All her attempts to shift the cuff and allow the shackle to be loose enough to slip off had been in vain, though. So all she could do was sit here and wait.

"I wish they hadn't nailed the beds to the floor," Herja said from beside her. "I thought we'd be able to drag them back together."

"We can't," Penelope said, harsher than she meant to.

Herja shot her an annoyed look.

Penelope closed her eyes and took a few deep breaths, regulating herself. "I'm sorry. I shouldn't have snapped."

"I understand why you did," Herja murmured.

"I still should have been calmer," Penelope replied. She rolled her tight shoulders and tried to stretch out the kink in her back. "I know that we're all just trying to figure out how we can fix this. But I don't think we can. We just have to wait it out."

If they made too much noise, the guards came back in. When Nolen tried to break his headboard last time, they warned the students that causing trouble would result in them being separated and sent to different towers, as ordered by Rowena.

"I know it feels hopeless," Kaia said, "but we have to keep positive. Rowena is smart, and she's not like her father. She'll figure out what Silas is actually doing and help us stop him."

"I hope you're right," Wickham murmured.

Penelope adjusted her position on the bed so she could lie down. It was highly uncomfortable, with her arm shackled at an odd angle, but she could adjust her position so it wasn't pulling so hard on her arm.

She had had a restless sleep the previous night, and it wasn't even noon yet. She needed to get some rest, even if she didn't sleep. Her gut churned, though—could they really trust Rowena? Was she different from her father, or was that just a role she played to put Odentia in a better position to deal with Eldavon?

Finnegan had tried to steal magic before, and now he was a dragon. How could they believe Rowena had a significant difference in her mindset than he did?

Not that they had much of a choice in the matter. They were prisoners here, just like last year with Lyra. Only this was even worse. It was just the six of them rather than the entire year with their classmates. They no longer had their dragons. Odentia wasn't a long-time ally of Eldavon, unlike Lyra.

The odds were stacked against them. Although in this case, there was a more clear-cut villain for them to fight against. Maybe they could find out what Silas actually wanted and convince him there were other ways to go about achieving his goals.

The door opened. Penelope jerked up so fast it yanked her arm, causing it to pop. She bit down on her cry of pain as she twisted to look at the door.

Rowena came in, her hands clasped in front of her, while Silas walked behind her. He'd removed his armor and was now dressed in floor-length robes. They were a rich blend of red and gold, with a trim along the hems that were embroidered with black, rune-like patterns.

If he had been gray instead of red and gold, and if he wore a veil over his face, he would look like the gorgon spirits she and Raven had seen in the Thunder Springs.

"Row—I mean, your Majesty," Kaia said. She got off her bed and curtsied awkwardly toward Rowena. "What's happening?"

Rowena lifted her chin, her gaze skimming over all of them. Her eyes held no emotion.

"I have listened to Silas' words, and I have found a great deal of wisdom in them." Rowena lowered her hands to her side. "You will all remain here as my prisoners."

"But you can't," Kaia yelped.

"I can—but I'm not cruel like my father," she added, focusing on Kaia again. "Although you are my prisoners, I will allow you all to decide whether you stay here, shackled to your beds, with a rotation schedule where one of you may be free to move about every hour—but only one at a time."

Penelope laughed. "That's supposed to be not cruel?"

"Or I can put you all into individual cells in the dungeons, like Kiango, Saffron, Hazel, and Henri," Rowena said. She cocked an eyebrow. "Which would you prefer?"

Penelope pressed her lips together tightly.

"That's what I thought," Rowena said. "I will also break my marriage to Hector. He will be kept in the towers. Comfortably, since he was kind to me, but he may not leave, either."

"But—" Kaia started.

Silas stepped forward, waving his hand dramatically at her. "Be silent! The queen does not need to hear your foolish protests."

Kaia ignored him. "But we're friends!"

"I warned you—"

"Silas, please." Rowena rested her hand on his arm, and he backed up a step, glaring at Kaia, though Penelope saw his eyes flicker hostilely toward Rowena. "We were never friends, Kaia. I was playing Eldavon's game so that your kingdom would stop holding everything you have over my head."

Kaia sank back onto the bed, betrayal written over her face.

"Everything I have done has been for protecting Odentia. And now I have the strength to do more than just protect her; I can make her thrive." Rowena shook her head, the blank look on her face moving to frustration now. "You would do the same if our positions were changed."

Penelope couldn't help but wonder if that was true and if she really would take such extreme measures if the situation was reversed.

"What's going to happen now?" she asked quietly.

"You will be kept here," Rowena repeated. "And so long as you obey my orders, you will not be harmed. I have no desire for any of you to be hurt. I'm just doing what I need to do for Odentia."

There seemed to be a layer to her voice. Penelope frowned, trying to figure it out.

"There has to be another way," Kaia whispered. "Something that makes it so we don't have to stay like this."

Rowena opened her mouth, but before she could say anything, Silas laughed.

"Actually," he said, raising his hands, "there is."

⁂

"Wait," Herja called, her heart in her throat.

Silas ignored her as he reached into his robes and withdrew a small orb. He held it aloft as a golden-silver light danced in its depths.

"Wait," Herja said again. "We won't—"

"What are you doing?" Rowena demanded, backing away from Silas.

Silas' grin widened. "I am doing what I must, your Majesty, to ensure these clever, oily children don't ruin everything."

Light arced from the orb. It shot forward, like grasping hands, and wrapped around Wickham, Herja, and Raven. Herja fought against the shackle holding her in place. If she had had a knife, she would have cut it off so she could tackle Silas. A howl ripped from her throat, and she tried desperately to catch any sense of her dragon still inside of her —but nothing happened.

Nothing at all.

The light wrapped around them, sinking into their skin. Kaia and Wickham both cried out at once, with Raven echoing them seconds later. They slumped to their beds, sweat breaking out over their skin. Herja screamed again while Penelope and Nolen both lunged so hard that they flipped around, their arms jerking them back.

"I can't watch this," Rowena cried and hurried from the room.

As soon as the door shut behind her, the smile on Silas' face dropped. He snorted as he glared at the door, then turned back to the students as an arrogant expression twisted his face.

"Consider yourselves lucky that she's so tender-hearted," Silas murmured as he tucked the orb back into his robes. "But thanks to her, if you all cooperate, then you won't have to get hurt. Think about that and decide what your lives are worth."

Herja bared her teeth but remained silent. Trying to fight back when in chains would not work—no, they needed to bide their time and get more information first.

Silas smiled at them now, apparently enjoying their silence. He strutted between the beds, checking on his work. He stopped at Raven and cocked his head to one side. "I'm glad to have you. I haven't been able to successfully transfer a witch's magic just yet. I'll start with the adults. Don't worry, but you three will make good backups."

He grinned at Wickham and Kaia, then turned on his heel and headed back for the door.

"Why are you doing this?" Kaia demanded.

"I'm not interested in telling my plans to you."

Herja pressed her fingers to her temples, holding in her own shouts. Because while the others were trying to get answers, something else had occurred to her... he called Raven a witch. He didn't realize they were a gorgon, not a witch. This meant he didn't know how they activated the mirrors...

Rowena and Finnegan would tell him the truth soon enough. But in the meantime, perhaps Raven being a gorgon would be enough to give them the edge they needed.

"Eldavon will see you brought down," she said, lifting her voice above the others. "We have ancient artifacts, as well as you. You might have that orb, the gorgon mirrors, but we have our own as well. We used them to retrieve Penelope and Rowena from you once—we'll use them to defeat you again."

Silas turned to her, a delighted look on his face. "Thank you for telling me how you did that. But don't worry—I'll retrieve all the artifacts of power from your pathetic kingdom soon enough. And once I have what I want—"

He cut himself off, shooting a nervous look at the door.

Triumph spread over Herja's face, so she spun it away so Silas wouldn't see.

So she was right! Silas didn't know they had a gorgon, and he was using ancient artifacts to do all this magic. And that look he'd given the door? Clearly, he was in it for his own ends and was spinning the whole 'restoration of balance' tale to blind the Odentian queen.

So did he use an artifact to artificially cause this drought as well? she wondered.

The door opened again, and Herja schooled her expression to peek back. Rowena entered, her face pale. Her hands clutched together as her eyes darted over them all.

"What did you do?" she asked Silas.

Silas sunk into a half-bow toward her. "I merely locked their magic, your Majesty. So they cannot cause you any trouble."

She licked her lips. "So I can have them freed from these shackles, and they can't send any warnings to Eldavon?"

"I... suppose so," Silas said doubtfully. "But I would not think that they deserved such—"

"They are not at fault for their kingdom's sins," Rowena interrupted. She reached for Silas' hand and beamed at him. "I'm glad to know you can bind their magic, though. It gives me a great deal of reassurance. I'll have them unlocked but kept in here. In the meantime, you and I have a lot to discuss."

Was... was that flirting? Herja felt nauseated. She fought that back. Whatever Rowena did was her own problem. The students and Eldavon had their own issues.

The door shut once more.

"I thought she was going to have us unshackled," Nolen growled.

"She will," Kaia said, but she sounded exhausted and hopeless now.

Herja rubbed her arm. Now that they were gone, the pain was making itself known. She didn't dare say aloud what she had figured out just yet, though. Who knew if Silas and Rowena were on the other side of the door, listening?

"I just don't understand how she could so quickly flip like this," Penelope murmured. "He's the one that put us in the mirror. How can she believe anything he says?"

"Maybe she doesn't," Raven said.

They all turned to Raven. They were lying on their bed, the silver-gold bands of magic still around them. It had already dispersed with Kaia and Nolen.

"What do you mean?" Herja asked.

"I don't know. Not yet. But there is more to these events than are so easily divined."

Herja leaned against her headboard, mulling over Raven's words. So what exactly did that mean? She knew better than to ask. But it gave her hope. Perhaps Rowena wasn't as swayed by Silas as she appeared to be.

NINETEEN

Kaia sipped a little of the water Nolen had given her. She wasn't thirsty, but it would make him feel better, so she did it. Honestly, she probably was a little dehydrated. She sighed as she stared outside at the fresh snow falling once more. It should have been beautiful, but all she could feel was this knot of betrayal in her gut.

They had been freed from their shackles for just over an hour, and she was still reeling from everything that had happened.

"I think it's been long enough," Penelope said.

"You think so?" Herja asked, lowering her voice.

"The longer we wait, the more time we risk Silas finding out Raven is a gorgon, and we lose our opportunity," Penelope replied. "If we're going to contact the Crown, we need to do it now. They need to know what's going on here."

Kaia turned away from the window as she finished her water. She set the glass down and marched to Raven, holding out a hand. She couldn't reach her own magic, but Raven had tried a few things and apparently could still access theirs. Whatever Silas did, it wasn't effective against gorgons.

Raven took Kaia's hand, then snatched their hand back as she'd burned them. Kaia jumped, startled.

"Kaia and Wickham can't be part of the circle," Raven hissed.

"Why not?" Wickham asked.

Raven turned toward him. "Whatever magic Silas used on the two of you is still connected to him somehow. If we put you in the circle, he'll know I still have my magic."

Normally, Kaia would ask how Raven could know that—but Raven had a way about them. They understood these connections far better than anyone else Kaia knew. She nodded and stepped back, tucking her hands behind her back.

Raven, Penelope, Nolen, and Herja joined hands in a circle. They all closed their eyes and bowed their heads... but as the minutes passed, nothing happened.

Finally, they dropped their hands.

Rowena shook their head. "There isn't enough with just the four of us. We have to get out of here and closer to Eldavon if we're going to connect with the Crown."

"Great," Kaia murmured. She closed her eyes.

She still had a hard time believing what she thought was a friendship with Rowena was all a lie. But in their present circumstances, she couldn't believe that Rowena was a genuine friend, either. The fear of Silas taking her and Wickham's magic made her confused and unable to think.

Only one thought could keep breaking through, each time bolder than the last. The kingdoms were primed for war. People were going hungry. Odentia was the only kingdom to have brought in a good crop harvest. Eldavon had stores of food, but they were limited. Other kingdoms had food that would get them through the winter, most likely.

Silas had planned this all well. Kaia couldn't believe he'd just stepped in to coincide with the drought. No, she believed Herja's theory that he used some sort of artifact to change the weather patterns over the land.

The others were discussing various plans to escape when the door opened. They all fell silent together. When Finnegan swaggered into the room, Kaia hurried to stand with the knot of her friends. Her shoulders tensed.

"What are you doing here?" Penelope asked. Her tone was oddly calm and in control.

"To boast, of course. After five years of being thwarted by a bunch of kids, I finally have what I want," Finnegan said loudly. But even as he spoke, he tossed a bundle of cloth at Penelope. She caught it.

The cloth was interwoven with images of flowers and leaves—Herja's bookbag.

Kaia's eyes widened. What was Finnegan actually doing? She wasn't the only one that looked from the bag back to Finnegan. He jerked his chin toward the bag with a significant look at them.

"I'm finally a dragon. I wish I could have shown my brother how mighty I've become. But he's gone because of Eldavon. You didn't know that, did you?" he rambled, gesturing at the bag now.

"What are you—" Herja started.

"He could have been healed from his illness if you only shared magic," Finnegan yelled. He lowered his voice to a hiss. "Get in so I can get you out of here."

Kaia's jaw dropped.

"And now you'll be punished for your hoarding," Finnegan said, returning to his shout. "Oh, don't start crying—you're not the victim here. You've stood on your own pedestals for too long."

Could they trust him? Kaia wasn't sure what he'd get for lying to them. Would he really be trying to rescue them? She strode forward, reaching for the bag in Penelope's hands. No point in drowning in questions—they couldn't get out of here on their own.

They had little choice other than to trust him. The alternative was to sit around here waiting until Silas started screwing with their magic.

She laid the bag on the bed so it'd be easier to crawl into, then opened it as wide as she could. She squirmed her way inside and quickly knew that there wouldn't be enough room for them all in there. As Wickham's face appeared at the entrance, she rolled a barrel of food toward him. He pulled it out, and Kaia rolled a second barrel.

All the while, Finnegan waxed on about what he was going to do now that he was a dragon. The others moved quickly, and soon the bag had been emptied of everything except one barrel of water, Herja's books, and the self-cleaning chamber pot. Then the other five wormed their way inside.

It was tight and claustrophobic with the six of them in the small space, but after some moving around, they could fit fairly comfortably.

Finnegan closed the opening. They jostled and swayed as Finnegan said, "And don't think your kingdom will fare any better!"

The sound of a door slamming made Kaia wince.

"Nobody is to go in or out of this room without the queen's direct permission," Finnegan said, presumably to a guard. "No food or water. They can think about where their loyalties lie as they starve."

"Yes, your grace," a deep voice responded.

Kaia closed her eyes as they swayed back and forth, hoping that they had made the right choice.

After what seemed like far too much time, the bag opened again. A blast of cold air swirled into the space, but Herja welcomed it. She sucked it in greedily, as Penelope was the first to work her way out. They had been crammed together for hours; the air was stuffy and hot, and Herja was more than eager for the cold air outside of the bag.

"When we get back to Eldavon, I'm going to get this expanded again," Herja muttered as she finally got her turn to crawl out. Her feet and hands were asleep from the way she'd been cramped on her side, but the cool, clean air instantly made her feel better.

Finnegan was nearby, setting up a lean-to tent over a small fire. They were in the woods,

"I need the bathroom," Kaia said, stumbling toward the trees.

The rest of them scattered to other areas, and once she felt she could walk without losing her balance, Herja joined them. By the time she was done and returned, the others had come back. And she was shivering. The snow falling all about them melted in her hair and against her thin shirt.

The six students huddled around the fire while Finnegan put up more canvases to close it in as a makeshift tent.

"Thank you," Kaia said to him as she held her hands to the fire.

Finnegan looked startled, then nodded to her. "You're, er, welcome, I guess."

Herja stretched her back and rotated her shoulders to ease her stiff muscles. She watched Finnegan suspiciously. His movements seemed stiff somehow like he wasn't entirely certain what he was doing. Or like he was feeling very awkward with them.

"So you got us away from Odentia's palace?" she asked, squinting.

"I did."

"Why?"

Finnegan finished tying the last canvas and returned to the fire. He brushed the snow off the ground and took a seat, staring into the fire. "It wasn't exactly my idea. Rowena thought it was for the best. Silas was speaking all about the glory of Odentia and hyping her up... the way her father used to talk about himself. She wanted me to get you out of there so we can warn Eldavon."

Herja frowned at his words. "You think Silas had your brother's ear? And that's why he did what he did?"

"I don't know. The point is that Rowena decided it would be best if she stayed to monitor what Silas did and used me to get you six out of there. She's told him I'm taking a letter demanding surrender to Eldavon, so it'll be a while before he gets suspicious. That's the plan, anyway," Finnegan said grimly.

Kaia laughed aloud. "I knew it! I knew she wasn't acting like herself."

She might be relieved, but Herja only frowned deeper. "Why play along with him, though? Why not just arrest him and stop him from any of these plans?"

Finnegan ran a hand through his hair and gave her a look as though she was asking an obvious question."

"Ah," Herja said, nodding. "I understand."

"I don't," Nolen grumbled.

Herja turned to him. "Silas has the power to take the dragons from us and give them to other people. He has bound Wickham and Kaia's magics. We don't know what sort of powers he has or what he can do.

So if Rowena plays along with him, she can get more information, rather than if she took a stand against him and he..."

She trailed off, leaving it to Nolen's imagination what Silas might do to take charge of Odentia without Rowena.

"The mirrors," Herja said.

Finnegan reached into his pack and pulled out Kaia's pouch. "Safe and sound. I figured you'd need them. Although I have no idea what we're going to do other than just get back to Eldavon."

"We should try to reach the crown," Herja said, grabbing Nolen and Raven's hands.

Raven took Finnegan's hand; he flinched but allowed it, then reluctantly took Penelope's hand when she held it out to him. Herja felt a nudge in her mind, the only sign that the connection had been formed. After a few minutes, Raven let out a grunt and shook their head.

"Still nothing."

"We'll try when we're closer," Herja said.

Kaia hugged her knees to her chest. "So we know Silas wants something with magic. But what? What is his plan?"

"From what I've seen, his plan is to use Odentia as his army so he can build his own power base and use Rowena as his shield and puppet, so he can have all the power with none of the risks," Finnegan said, his expression growing grimmer. "And it's clear that he's casting Eldavon as the villain to be destroyed to start Odentia's conquests."

CHAPTER

TWENTY

The next morning, Kaia and Nolen rode on Finnegan's back while the other four stayed in the book bag. The extra space made it easier for them to read Herja's books and find useful information to resolve the situation.

After a few hours, Finnegan touched down; Kaia and Nolen were freezing, so Penelope and Wickham switched places with them.

They flew the whole day, and when night arrived, they set up camp and foraged as much food as they could, but in the end, they had a weak broth made from boiling beef jerky. Finnegan got the actual meat, as he was the one using the most effort.

"It just feels hopeless," Wickham said as he held a wet shirt over the fire. It had gotten dirty, and he had washed it in the snow, but it wasn't drying as fast as he wanted. "I don't know why I thought this year would go any better than any of the others. Every year..."

He shook his head. He hated to be wrapped up in this self-pity party that he was caught in, but it was true. This situation was even worse than last year! Raven still couldn't connect with anyone in Eldavon. Could Silas' magic have restricted them after all?

It was never the fate of Eldavon on their shoulders before. And worse, too—this was about Odentia, and all of their neighboring kingdoms.

Kaia took his hand and squeezed it. "Eldavon isn't without friends. Silas will have to do more than take away our dragons to turn all the kingdoms against us."

"Which is why he's spinning that story about the drought being our fault," Wickham replied.

"Yes. But even those tensions aren't exactly because the kingdoms dislike Eldavon; it's fear about their needs not being met. We can't just fall into hopeless mindsets," Kaia said, looking around at all of them. Her expression was fierce. "I know we're in a critical situation, but once we think that the entire world is against us, we will have a harder time getting through this."

Finnegan's brows furrowed as he watched her. Wickham glared momentarily at the prince; he didn't like the attention Finnegan gave Kaia.

Kaia seemed to be oblivious. "This isn't about Eldavon anymore. It's about all the kingdoms. We're not more important than they are. We just have to restore balance. And maybe that means spreading magic outside of our kingdom. Maybe we have been holding too tightly. Worried about the very violence we face now."

Wickham sighed, distracted from Finnegan once more. "And that's something that's been building for a while. Regardless of our reasons for keeping magic to our people..."

"Other kingdoms saw it as holding back a power from them that would make their lives easier," Finnegan murmured. His gaze had shifted to Wickham now. "I know because I felt the same way, too. I thought I could be a savior for Odentia."

"And now Silas is positioning himself to fill that savior position," Herja said. She had a book on her lap, but apparently, the conversation was too much for her to concentrate on.

"Exactly," Finnegan replied. He shifted on the spot and stared into the forest. Hearing him talk, I'm sure he was working on my brother before his death. He knew too much. I'm certain he was manipulating my brother to increase the tension between Odentia and Eldavon.

Herja sighed. "Which means we can't act rashly, not when Silas has had so much time to plot his advance here."

They all fell silent once more. Wickham hated that right now; all they really could do was talk about the situation. He wanted to do something. But his mind ran in too tight of circles to read, and their chief concern was to get back to Eldavon. They didn't dare try to use the gorgon mirrors without knowing more about how they worked.

They needed a plan. And right now, the only plan was to get to Eldavon. Finnegan had been flying all day; it wasn't workable for him to continue to fly at night, which was why they were making this food. And then he'd sleep in the bookbag while the students continued on foot until morning.

"We should get moving again soon," Penelope said. "We'll do our best to gather more food while we're on the move."

"We should switch this up so that we're on foot during the day and flighting at night," Herja said. "So we have daylight to forage. Not that it will do much good when we're sludging through so much snow."

Nolen lifted his head. "Regardless, we should get moving soon. We can figure out if we need to switch things up while we're on the move."

Wickham nodded. "The sooner we can get to Eldavon, the better. I'm willing to go hungry for a few days so we can get there faster. As Kaia said, this isn't about us anymore. It's far bigger than that."

Penelope pulled her jacket tighter around herself as a stiff wind blew up, cutting through her as it threw wet snow from the trees down on her. Herja had a point about switching the nights and days. While they couldn't fly on Finnegan's back in this sort of weather, at least during the day, they'd be a little warmer.

The light stone lantern she held lit up the path ahead. It was difficult going, moving through the forest while avoiding the pitfalls that were hidden by the deep snow. At least they had a starless night, allowing her to know they were moving in the right direction.

"Is everyone doing all right?" she called over her shoulder. They were walking single-file, with Herja at the back of the group.

"Yes," replied her classmates. They all sounded exhausted.

Penelope had gone first in this case because she was most used to walking through snow, so it was easier for her to break the trail than it was for the others. She would have to switch with Nolen before too long, though. Her legs were feeling like blocks of wood.

A heavy weight settled over her. She didn't like being in this situation with no choice but to trust Finnegan.

Since he'd gotten Hector's dragon, he hadn't given them any reason not to trust him. Penelope wished she could read his mind to know if he was genuine.

Raven stepped around Nolen so they could walk right behind Penelope. "Do you need to talk?"

Penelope twisted slightly, checking to make sure Herja still had the book bag. She didn't want to risk Finnegan overhearing this. She kept her voice low to make sure it wouldn't carry.

"Have you had any prophecy dreams?"

Raven sighed, their veil fluttering with the force of it.

Penelope wished she had one, too, but Raven hadn't been able to keep any of the extra clothes they'd brought with them to Odentia. None of the students had.

"I might have," Raven whispered. "It's all been quite confusing. I keep seeing dragons in the sky, but they're made of puppets. I think it might represent this situation, but I can't be certain. I've been dreaming of the gray ones, too."

Grey ones. The ancient gorgons.

"What have they been telling you?" Penelope asked eagerly.

"Nothing. They've just been silent. We seem to stand on a spinning plate, perfectly balanced. I'm afraid to move, worried that I'll knock us off course and we'll fall and shatter. Then I look up, and there are puppet dragons in the sky, but then the sun crashes, and we all burn up."

Penelope flinched. That did not sound hopeful at all.

"I'm not sure it's a bad thing," Raven said, but they sounded doubtful. "I think it's more telling me that Silas is behind the unbalance of magic here. I'm not sure that you can say that Eldavon is 'hoarding' magic. Guarding it sounds better."

"Sounds better, yes," Penelope said. "But we think that things have changed. Isn't that what we've come up against with all our quests? Times have changed, and traditions and society need to adjust to those changes. I'm not entirely certain that Silas is wholly wrong... just his actions. Not necessarily what he's been saying."

Nolen made a disgruntled noise. "Are you serious right now?"

Penelope stopped walking and turned to him. "Unfortunately, yes. I'm not sure that it's a good thing to keep other kingdoms from drinking from the Silver Springs. We could share our knowledge."

Nolen's brow furrowed.

"Think about it. You're stubborn, right? You don't like to accept help?"

"Not really."

"But when will people help you learn how to take care of your own issues?" Penelope arched her brow. "Maybe that's what we're doing. We're putting other kingdoms in a position where they have to let us take care of them."

Nolen's expression cleared. "Oh."

Kaia spoke. "So you're saying, maybe they're not refusing the aid we offer them, maybe they just see it as a power struggle? Maybe they want to take care of themselves?"

"Yeah. I think that might be part of it. But I know I don't have all the answers here. I know we can't make that choice ourselves—we need to get to Eldavon. We need to warn them and stop Silas."

Penelope breathed in the cold air, pulling it into her lungs to clear her head. The philosophical questions and right and wrong were too much for her to resolve at this moment. She wasn't even sure if she was right. That other kingdoms saw the offer of aid as a power struggle just proved that they wouldn't know how to take care of magic properly. Didn't it?

"Do you need me to take point?" Nolen asked.

"Yeah. I am getting tired."

"I can carry the book bag, Herja," Kaia offered.

"Thanks."

They continued on. Penelope's mind was in a whirl as they trudged in the darkness. Even if they opened up magic after this was resolved, it didn't take care of their current situation. If they failed in this, the consequences would be unthinkable.

But how were they going to resolve the situation? Was it even possible?

Raven took her hand and squeezed. Penelope squeezed back, bolstered by her mate's presence. They would figure something out. They had gotten out of seemingly impossible situations before. They just had to work together and do one step at a time.

An image swirled in her mind, those gorgon mirrors lying side-by-side. The bright light emitted from them. The cold gray mist that had filled her lungs and put her to sleep.

A shudder ran down Penelope's spine, and she forced herself not to think about it.

TWENTY-ONE

P enelope glanced at the darkening sky. They only had a couple of hours of daylight left and needed to get some food. Unfortunately, their rationing hadn't gone as planned, as they were running out faster than they expected.

They were close to the border to Eldavon, however. Penelope turned to Raven; they had already tried to reach out to the Crown and said they almost felt like they could. "Do you think you could do it if Kaia and Wickham were included in the circle?"

"Wait, you said you couldn't do that," Finnegan said, lifting his head and frowning. He'd apparently not slept well today.

"We don't know if it will tip Silas off to our location," Penelope explained. "But if we can warn the Crown, it might be worth it."

Raven hummed. "I'm not sure. I feel like there might be something else going on rather than just distance. I—"

Penelope whirled to her feet as three men came through the trees. They wore the uniforms that Odentian warriors wore, except there had been a patch added with the image of what looked like a flowering staff. Their eyes glowed silver, and Penelope's heart jumped to her throat.

"Look what we have here," one of them sneered. "If it isn't the little traitor prince and his Eldavon friends."

Finnegan leaped toward Raven. He grabbed their face veil and yanked hard. Raven cried out, holding it in place. Penelope surged toward them. She punched Finnegan in the side, a bellow in her throat. What did he think he was doing?

The warriors laughed as Penelope dragged Finnegan off Raven.

"They're dragons," Finnegan howled.

Penelope didn't respond, still fighting to hold him. Her teeth were bared in a fierce snarl—she would not let Finnegan use Raven as a weapon!

"Look at that," the same warrior as before taunted. "They aren't very smart, are they? Just playing games with each other. The queen wants you all back alive. I don't know why but if you behave yourselves, we might just obey those orders."

Kaia burst into tears. She dropped to her knees, pressing her face to her hands. Penelope stopped fighting with Finnegan, staring at her in surprise. She had never seen Kaia break down like this!

The others all looked shocked—including the warriors.

"I want to go home," she sobbed. "Please, just let me go home!"

The warrior scoffed, drawing himself up while the one to his right looked uncertain. "Get to your feet! If you think you can manipulate us, you have another thing coming."

Kaia staggered back to her feet, then stumbled to one side as though she were trying to run away. Then she stopped.

"What are you doing?" Finnegan demanded.

"I want to go home!"

Everybody's eyes were on her. *Everybody*.

Penelope inched toward the fire where Herja's bookbag was. The warriors were too busy watching Finnegan and Kaia to pay attention. With her heart in her throat, she moved slowly to pick up the bag, then inched back to Raven, Herja, and Wickham. Nolen had moved toward Kaia, but she waved her hand at him, still sobbing into the other one.

"Why are you doing this?" Kaia asked. "What did we do?"

"The queen's orders," the warrior replied, sounding a little lost now.

Penelope opened the bag as wide as it would, still watching the warriors. They must not be well trained if they are so easily distracted. "Get in," she whispered.

Wickham and Herja gave her wild looks, but Raven stepped into the bag, sliding in easily. Herja went next, and finally Wickham. That meant they only needed Kaia and Nolen. Penelope moved forward, trying to keep herself unnoticeable. One warrior glanced at her, and she froze.

The warrior squinted with his hand on his weapon. "Quit letting her delay us. We have to get going."

Finnegan rolled to the balls of his feet. "You seem to think I'll be going without a fight."

The attention focused on him. Penelope quickly hissed to Nolen to get into the bag, which he did. Now Kaia. Penelope skirted around Finnegan, risking the attention drawn to her once more. As she came to stand beside Kaia, the first warrior let out a startled cry.

"Hey! Where did the others go?"

Penelope yanked the bag open, shouting, "Get in!"

Kaia dove headfirst; she briefly became stuck, but the others must have pulled her in, and she disappeared. Penelope quickly hopped in with both feet, praying this would work. Even before she landed on the wooden flooring with a thud, a giant clawed hand had caught the bag, and they were off, bumping into each other as they swung through the air.

Herja groaned as she crawled out of the book bag. The six of them had been crammed in there so tightly that it took them far too long to get organized, so they each had a little space. Her heart was hammering, and she felt like she would be sick.

She crawled some distance from the bag and rolled onto her back, breathing deeply as she stared at the dark sky. A gentle misting rain fell on her face, easing her stomach churning.

The others also came out; Herja had to fight back a swell of jealousy as Penelope and Kaia immediately made camp. How could they have gone through the same thing as she did and still be able just immediately to get to work? It didn't seem fair.

Still, Herja pulled herself together shortly after. Finnegan was exhausted, so he slept while the students ventured into the cold forest to gather what food they could find. Herja was shivering badly when she got back and only had a handful of nuts as her reward for the effort.

The six of them sat around the fire, cooking their meager meal. Eventually, Finnegan got up and joined them.

"I don't suppose they told you how they found us?" Herja asked him.

Finnegan shook his head. There were dark circles under his eyes. "They said that Rowena and Silas have moved to Eldavon, though. They said something about the Eldavon throne already belonging to her, and they were ordered to take us there rather than back to the Odentian palace."

Herja flinched. That was not good.

"So we need more information," Kaia said. "How do we get it? Go into town and ask questions? We need more food, too."

Finnegan frowned at her. "After that breakdown you had, I'm not sure it's a good idea."

Kaia lifted her head. She gave him an incredulous look as she folded her arms. "I was faking. I needed to keep their attention on me and off the others so they could get into the bag without being noticed. And I think you'll find that it worked."

"Oh." Finnegan still gave her a puzzled sort of look.

Herja cleared her throat. "She's right. We need more information and food. So we'll have to go to the nearest town. But first, we need a plan."

Kaia stretched out her back as she slid off the bar stool, leaving her untouched glass of wine behind. The bartender hadn't even tried to get any sort of proof of age from her. Whether it was poor practices from the bar or if Odentia's laws about alcohol differed from Eldavon, she didn't know. All she knew was that this had been the cheapest item she could order.

Between the seven of them, they'd scraped up enough money to buy some supplies. They were also being forced to sell some of Herja's precious books... Kaia's heart clenched for her. Herja had tried to put on a brave face, but it had clearly hurt her.

Nobody paid much mind to Kaia as she slipped from the bar. She caught her reflection in the window briefly and held in a shudder. They had dyed her and Wickham's hair with nut husks, turning them both brunette.

Brown hair didn't suit her. She missed her own silver curls.

But oh well. Her hair would grow out, and she would have stood out too much with her natural hair. She could overhear a conversation in the bar, which gave her more information than they'd had since they left the Institute.

Nolen was waiting for her at the previously decided spot. They fell in step together, and Kaia waited until the surrounding crowds had dispersed before she spoke.

"It's worse than we thought," she murmured. "Finnegan was right. Rowena and Silas have gone to the Eldavon palace; she has now declared herself queen of the kingdom. I couldn't find anything about the Crown. But Silas won't have hurt them, will he?"

She looked up at Nolen, searching his expression for reassurance. He put his arm around her waist, pulling her closer, but was silent. He was nervous and kept looking around as if he thought guards might appear out of nowhere.

"Several of the other kingdoms have declared war on Eldavon but repealed it as soon as Rowena declared herself queen," Kaia continued. "So that's a good thing, right? Although I suppose they're only stopping because they're afraid of dragons."

"I don't now. Maybe. I don't like the idea of Rowena sweeping in and making herself queen, though. Are we sure she's not just hedging her bets with us? She could be genuine in wanting this power."

Kaia sighed. "It's possible, but we've spent time with her. I don't think it's in her personality."

"Maybe not."

Kaia leaned against him, chewing her lip. She'd picked up more information but wasn't sure it was a good idea to keep talking here. Nolen was already tense, and the information she had gathered would make him even more tense. She wanted him to know, though, so that he could share this information with the others if, for any reason, she was delayed.

After the dragons confronted them in the woods, she felt there were far more risks in this situation than any of them realized.

They bumped into a woman carrying a baby, and Nolen pulled Kaia aside, glaring at the woman. She ducked her head and scurried away, but it drew the attention of several people around them. They started taking notice of Nolen, no doubt because his scowl was so fierce. A few of them glanced at her and back at him, as though worried about her safety.

"Come here," Kaia said, grabbing his hand.

She pulled him into a little alleyway, away from the crowds. The alley was cramped and dirty, but when she pulled him into her arms, he dropped his head to her shoulder.

"I'm sorry," he murmured. "I just want to get you out of here and back to safety."

"I know," Kaia murmured back to him. She rubbed his back; some people on the street kept watching them. "Shake your shoulders as though you're crying."

Nolen made a noise but did so. Kaia rested her cheek against his head and continued rubbing his back in small circles, like she was comforting him. The people watching slowly looked away.

She doubted they'd be so concerned about her if she were actually threatened.

"Several of Eldavon's allies are remanding Rowena to return to Odentia," Kaia murmured in Nolen's ear. "Mermaids and krakens have been reported displaying aggression towards the fleets of other kingdoms, too. If this dissolves into war, it'll be far bigger than any we've dealt with."

Nolen held her tighter. "I heard information, too."

Kaia tensed. Nolen's voice cracked, betraying his emotion. His shoulders shook ahead, real now instead of being for show.

"Everyone at the Institute has been moved to the Palace and jailed. Everyone, even the first years."

Cold drenched Kaia's body. Why would Rowena do that? Even if she was only playing along with Silas, it gave him access to the other witches to experiment on. The faces of her classmates flashed through her mind. Were they safe in those dungeons? Or would they be Silas's next victims?

CHAPTER
TWENTY-TWO

Wickham handed a few of their precious coins to the vendor for a whole chicken. It was a scrawny bird, but it was also the largest he could afford then. For the six of them, it'd make one, maybe two meals, but they could also boil the bones and get sustenance from the broth. It was better than nothing. He longed to buy a few of the carrots and make vegetable stock, but unfortunately, they were even more expensive.

"Thank you," he told the vendor.

The vendor smiled and nodded back at him. "If you're looking for work, check out the bulletin board over there," she said, pointing. "There's always odd jobs that travelers like yourself can find for a few extra coins."

Wickham nodded his thanks, blushing. No doubt she noticed him gazing longingly at the fresh produce. Some quick jobs might be just what they needed, though.

He headed over just as a guard was finishing tacking up a poster. Wickham patiently waited his turn, his gaze skimming the marketplace for Herja as he did so. She was at another vendor, bargaining for a few books in return for some heavy blankets they could use to keep warm.

The guard moved on, and Wickham stepped up to the bulletin board. His eyes were drawn to the poster that the guard had just tacked up and his heart dropped.

Staring back at him was his own face. The others were on there, too, and a large portrait of Finnegan. His jaw worked as he read the lines. *Wanted, alive, and unharmed. Witches of Eldavon who have stolen the mind of our beloved Prince. They absolutely must not be harmed under penalty of death. $200 reward for credible information, $1000 reward per person arrested.*

Great. He reached to yank it down, but he couldn't do that. It'd draw even more attention to himself. He looked around quickly and saw a handful of town guards around. They weren't looking at him— the image of him was clean-shaven with long hair, and he'd cut it and used it to create a false mustache.

They were slowly converging on Herja.

Striding forward, he made a beeline for Herja and grabbed her hand. She made a startled noise as he attempted to put the books back in her bag with one hand.

"Wick, what are you doing?"

The guards jumped into action, rushing toward them.

"Run!" Wickham shouted.

He yanked on Herja's hand, abandoning the books. She grabbed one of the hanging blankets, ripping it from its hanger. The vendor let out a shout, and then they were gone. The guards leaped in their way, and Wickham ducked, ramming one with his shoulder. Herja kicked out the feet of the other, and they rushed away from the marketplace.

The guards scrambled to their feet and raced after them.

"No weapons," he heard someone bellow behind them. "They're wanted alive!"

"What?" Herja gasped. She pulled on Wickham's hand, pulling him down an alley. There was an open window, and she crawled through it, Wickham coming after. They slammed the window shut just as the clatter of footsteps sounded outside, and they dropped, hiding just below the window.

Wickham's heart pounded in his throat, but the guards moved on quickly. He peered around the room; it was empty save for a bed and wardrobe. Either someone had left the window open and forgotten about it, or this town saw little crime. He assumed the latter, considering how easy it had been to escape the guards.

"What's going on?" Herja whispered to him, her eyes wide.

"Rowena's sent out wanted posters for us," Wickham replied in a whisper.

Herja's eyes closed.

"We have to warn the others, but the guards know what we look like and what we're wearing." His heart sank. How were they supposed to get out of this?

"How is your magic? Is it still locked?"

Wickham lifted his hands. On the one hand, yes, it felt like something was in the way. On the other hand, he could sense more energy around him than usual. "I'm not sure."

"No changing our hair, then," she muttered. She shook her head as she carefully closed the curtains to the window and tiptoed to the wardrobe. It was filled with dresses.

"Get changed," she said, pulling out the tallest dresses. She grimaced as she tossed it to him. "You need to stay hidden. So, the mustache goes, and here's a shawl you can use to cover your hair.

Wickham took off his outer clothes and put them in the burlap sack along with his chicken, which he tied about his waist before he pulled on the dress. It fit, though barely. His shoulders pressed at the seams while the skirt was mid-calf. He looked into the mirror when he folded the shawl over his head.

He didn't look half-bad. So long as nobody looked at him too closely, he could work the dress with his lanky frame. It was good that he'd always been just a little small for his age.

By this time, Herja was struggling to take off a dress that was too tight across her chest. Wickham helped her remove it, but as she grunted in annoyance, Wickham picked up her clothes and turned them inside out. The lining was a duller color than the outside, so that should help her hide a bit more. Once she put her clothes back on inside out, he pressed his facial mustache under her lip.

"There," he said, "we both look different."

Herja wrinkled her nose but nodded. "You get to the mapmakers. I'll find Kaia and Nolen."

"Be careful," Wickham breathed.

They kissed and then slipped out the window again, heading in opposite directions. Wickham moved awkwardly, hoping that he wouldn't draw too much attention. The dress felt odd in how it clung to his body, and the loose skirt allowed cold air to billow in against his legs. He didn't understand why Kaia loved dresses so much.

Luckily, nobody paid him much mind as he moved through the town. He kept thinking someone was about to shout, 'Hey, that's my dress!' but he found Penelope and Raven easily. It occurred to him as he approached that the two of them had been featured together on the poster.

"We have to go," he murmured, sidling up to Raven. Now would be the time when mind-to-mind communication would come in handy!

Raven's head turned toward him. Even with their face covered, he could see the double take.

"Pen," Raven called. Penelope was currently arguing with the mapmaker over what Wickham didn't know.

Penelope turned and did the same double take of Wickham.

"We have taken up too much of this gentleman's time," Raven said, their voice low and soothing. "Willa here says that Mama has supper ready. We should get back to camp."

"A-alright," Penelope stammered.

The three of them headed out of town swiftly. Wickham explained what happened under his breath, and Penelope let out a shaky growl.

"You two get back to camp and Finnegan," she said.

They had left Finnegan in the forest because he would most likely be recognized. At least, he used to be.

Wickham nodded. "What about you?"

"I'll go back to help Herja, Nolen, and Kaia," she said.

Raven cocked their head and nodded. "They'll need it. Be careful, Pen. The last thing we can do is host a prison break."

Penelope grinned at her mate. "Don't worry. I'll be back before you know it."

She spun around and headed back into town, her blazing red hair sure to draw all the attention. As Wickham and Raven continued, he couldn't help but look over his shoulder, wincing. Was this really a good idea? Or should Penelope have stayed with them?

Raven said it was a good idea, he thought, steeling himself. *And Raven knows best about these things.*

Herja panted, her fake mustache on her chin. Her limbs ached from fending off the guards' batons with the garden hoe she had grabbed. The sharp blade on the end made it a more deadly weapon than she knew she should have. Regardless of what those wanted posters said, the guards would kill to defend themselves...

"Give it up, girl," the guard she faced spat. A nasty bruise was rising on his cheek as he glared at her.

Another guard went for Kaia behind them, and Nolen sidestepped, swinging his own stick at the guard. The guard leapt back, and Herja hissed.

"Stay in formation," she snapped.

The three of them circled, their backs to each other, as the guards wove back and forth. They kept going for Kaia, clearly seeing her as their weak spot. Kaia was holding her own for now, but Nolen kept dodging back to help her, leaving Herja's back exposed.

A crowd was gathering around them. Herja saw a flicker of red that disappeared as quickly as she saw it. She ground her teeth as the guards drew in thicker around them. She gripped the hoe tighter as her eyes roved around them, searching for any way to escape. They hemmed the group in tightly on all sides.

A figure stepped from the crowd. They were draped in a long fabric sheet over their head, belted at the waist with the sides rolled inward. Herja's eyes widened.

"Raven?" she cried.

"Yes," the figure said—in Penelope's voice.

Herja remembered the flash of red. She nearly grinned but forced herself to remain neutral-faced. "What are you doing here?"

"I saw you were in trouble, and I came to help," Penelope replied.

The lead guard had extracted himself from the others and glared up and down at Penelope. "And just what are you supposed to be?"

Penelope lifted a rolled paper in her hand and let it fall open. It was the wanted poster, but only the part with Raven. The words beneath it were written in large letters. *Approach with caution and do not reveal their face. The Gorgon is especially dangerous.*

"Do you know what a gorgon is?" Penelope asked, her voice musical as she let the poster drop.

The guard drew back. From the mutters of the others, they knew, too. The crowd slowly backed away from Penelope.

"I have no desire to harm any of you," Penelope said. "And the poster says no harm to me or my comrades under penalty of death. Let us leave or else I will reveal my face. You will all turn to stone, and poor Prince Finnegan... well. There is a reason we aren't to be harmed."

Herja gripped her weapon tighter, watching. Her heart beat in her throat. Would it work?

The leader fell back a step as his shoulders slumped. "Let them go."

There were mumbles among the others, but none seemed willing to face down a gorgon. Herja took a deep breath as she lowered the hoe. When none of the guards attempted to come after her, Kaia, or Nolen, she dropped it to the ground entirely. Then, she led the other two to Penelope.

"What are you even after?" the lead guard snapped at them as they made their way toward the distant forest, the townspeople edging away.

Herja paused. It was unlikely that any of these people would believe them, but they might as well tell the truth, right? "We're looking to stop a wicked sorcerer holding Rowena hostage and stealing the dragon forms from our people. Oh, and he's also stopped up the rains, so we want them back, too."

The lead guard's face twisted in confusion. Herja could only smile back—it really did sound impossible when she said it that way, didn't it?

CHAPTER
TWENTY-THREE

They flew north for two days, but every time they tried to get into a town to gather supplies, they found that the wanted posters were already there. After a discussion, the seven of them decided they wouldn't risk going into any town anymore, and they would work their way south again and try to skirt around to the Golden Forest, where they might find help from the Chameleon Sprites.

Wickham and Finnegan were out hunting a week after the encounter in town. The dress Wickham had worn to escape the Odentia town had been repurposed by Kaia, who used the fabric to sew everyone something to help keep them warm. For Wickham, it was a hat and a pair of mitts for his hands. He wondered about the dress's owner and hoped that whoever it was hadn't lost their favorite dress.

"You're surprisingly good at this," Finnegan said when Wickham had successfully killed a partridge to bring back-to-back.

Wickham arched a brow at him. "Why would you be surprised?"

"I haven't ever known a student of any sort to have experience hunting," Finnegan replied.

"I wasn't always a student. I grew up in a logging camp. We were always isolated and conscious of stretching the supplies from the Crown." Wickham shrugged. "After my baby sister was born, my parents decided to move to town. They saw how much I constantly worried and thought if I had more stability, it would make me worry less."

"Did it?"

Wickham couldn't help but laugh as he shook his head. "I always have to worry about something. If I don't, then I make something up, and it gets worse. But I learned how to hunt because I was worried we'd run out of food... even though we never did."

Finnegan nodded slowly as they continued, their bows in hand and the quivers of arrows at their hips for easy draw. "So that's how you managed to feed yourselves in the Silent Marshes, is it?"

"Partly," Wickham admitted. He hesitated, then shrugged. "For the most part, we were foraging plants. We constantly made marsh-weed soup with whatever bits of other things we could find. And I had my herbs that we used for seasoning."

"Resourceful." Finnegan stared ahead, a troubled look in his eyes. Finally, he glanced at Wickham and shrugged. "I'm sorry about that, by the way. You kids didn't deserve to be hunted. I convinced myself that you weren't kids at all. It's not an excuse, though. I'm sorry."

Wickham took a moment to rest, scanning the snow-covered ground as he did so. Despite his makeshift hat, his ears were freezing. They should head back to camp soon. Still, this conversation with Finnegan was easier than he had expected. He was more open than Nolen was.

"How did you get so far into Eldavon, anyway? You and all your warriors got to Mount Eldavon one year and then the Silent Marshes the next without being stopped. How?"

Finnegan sighed. "The mirror that you six came through from the Institute. My brother had a potion in a bottle. He refused to say where he got it from—Silas, no doubt—that he used to activate it. He said it could get us to wherever we needed to be."

Wickham frowned. "But it couldn't have been to wherever. Otherwise, why didn't you just go straight to the Silver Springs?"

"There were limitations, but my brother would never have admitted that. So, he said we have to work to get hostages and refused to hear anything else. And I was too afraid of him to talk back." Finnegan's expression darkened as his eyes took a far-away look.

"Then, when I was sent back to Eldavon for Kaia's offer to live with the Chameleon Sprites, he told me to find the sword I took. He told me how to get to the springs on Thunder Ridge," he continued. Then he shook his head and pushed against the tree he was leaning on. "It's getting dark; we should get back to camp."

"Yeah," Wickham agreed.

They turned back and followed the lines in the snow they had forged, with Finnegan walking ahead again. Wickham considered the things that he had just learned here. It seemed that Finnegan was truly remorseful—which Wickham had already believed, but it was nice to have an apology.

"It really does seem like your brother was working with Silas," he said slowly, shaking his head. "I guess we'll never really know why he targeted Odentia, though, will we?"

"Probably not," Finnegan agreed.

The snow crunched beneath Wickham's feet, and the dead partridge weighed down on one side. He remembered how Finnegan was when they encountered him on the Thunder Ridge, coughing, wheezing, showing signs of chronic malnourishment.

"You said you think Silas killed your brother?" Wickham said after a few minutes. "Did you want to talk about it?"

Finnegan shook his head. "He was in good health, and then he was dead. What am I supposed to think?"

"I... suppose there is merit to that. But I'm not sure if you want to talk about it or not. You shook your head, but you still said..." Wickham trailed off as Finnegan turned around.

"What does it matter?"

Wickham shrugged. Truthfully, he felt the brotherly concern he'd grown up with and the need to care for a patient he often felt. It was odd, considering that Finnegan was older than he was. But Wickham was a big brother. He knew how big brothers were meant to look after their younger siblings.

Something that Finnegan's brother surely had not done.

"I know you suffered from chronic illness because of your malnour-ishment," Wickham replied, bolstering himself. He hoped Finnegan wouldn't get angry with him. "And I know it's because of your brother's actions. He's old enough that your niece is barely younger than you are. He should have looked after you and protected you."

"My brother was not a good man," Finnegan replied. He snorted and turned back to the trail. "And even though he's been dead for two years, I still don't feel safe saying it. And even though I know he wasn't a good man..."

He trailed off, but Wickham could guess what he would say. Even though he wasn't good, Finnegan still wished he could have had his brother's love and affection. It was a natural reaction that Finnegan's brother had taken advantage of.

"You didn't deserve to be treated that way."

They were out of the trees now, and Wickham picked up his pace to walk alongside Finnegan. They were in the rolling hills just east of a stately mountain range that divided the border between Eldavon and Odentia. Here, large herds of bison had pushed back the forest, allowing the hills to be covered in tall, swaying grasses.

The grass was buried under a foot of snow, but the unexpected air pockets beneath the crust made Wickham careful in choosing where to put his feet.

"I didn't deserve it," Finnegan murmured. He let out a bitter laugh. "I never know what to expect with you Eldavon kids. I literally tried to kill your friend in the marshes. I wasn't just trying to bluff. I would have killed Kaia."

Wickham stopped and reached out to grab Finnegan's arm, pulling him to a stop as well. "I know."

"Then how can you possibly say..." Finnegan lifted both his hands into the air and let them drop again.

"I know. It's weird. But we understand better why you did what you did and where your mind frame was. Do I think it's excusable? No. But I also think people can change, and you've done a heck of a lot to prove that you have."

Finnegan let out a ragged breath. "You're all still weird."

Wickham laughed.

"I wouldn't have changed if it wasn't for Rowena." Finnegan turned his face toward the sky. "When she was born, her mother and she were both put into the tower with me. My brother, at that time, had suffered an accident that prevented him from having children. Rowena would be his only heir. Her mother got sick. I ended up raising her, more or less. There were nannies. None that stayed long."

Wickham looked toward the sky as well. The darkness was so complete that Wickham couldn't even see the stars. Though he longed for more light, he also knew the cloud cover would hold in more of the sparse heat they'd received during the day. A clear night was an even colder night.

"It was only after my brother was dead and I realized how he had treated Rowena that I looked at my actions. To see how I had behaved and how wicked I truly was."

"You did change, though."

"For Rowena. She's the best that Odentia offers."

Wickham nodded and walked again. "You have changed, Finnegan. And that's why we can forgive you for your behavior. Because regardless of the reasons you changed, you have attempted to prove yourself. So maybe it's time you start forgiving yourself, too."

Finnegan trudged behind him. After a long moment, he whispered, "I'm not sure that's possible."

Wickham turned again, but Finnegan brushed past him and quickened their pace.

"Let's get back to camp," he said gruffly, and Wickham knew this subject was closed.

⁂

Despite the howling wind outside, the space within the book bag was snug and warm. Kaia, Penelope, and Raven were inside. Kaia and Raven worked to mend some clothes while Penelope read one of Herja's books. It wouldn't be long before they traded space with Wickham, Nolen, and Herja. Finnegan insisted he could use his fires to keep himself warm, but the six students suffered in the cold.

"I think I can use my magic again," Kaia said, looking up from her needle.

Penelope grunted. She was stretched out on her stomach, her finger pressed against the book's page as she read.

"Can you make these clothes warmer?" Raven asked. They sounded exhausted—which was no surprise. Everyone was exhausted but still too wound up in the situation to feel like they could get proper sleep.

"I was thinking more about using a sleeping spell on you," Kaia replied. "If you can sleep for a solid amount of time, we might get a dream or two that will be useful in... all this," she said, waving her hand as though to encapsulate the world.

This got Penelope's attention. She lifted her head, her eyes looking slightly glazed. "What are you talking about?"

"Kaia thinks she can use her magic again," Raven said.

Penelope rolled to a sitting position. She got caught in the clothes Kaia was sewing as she did so, nearly yanking it from Kaia's hands.

"Hey," Kaia cried, startled.

"Sorry, sorry!" Penelope carefully detangled herself. "What do you mean? You can use magic again?"

Kaia sighed. "That's exactly what I mean. Silas's binding spell is fading."

"Are you sure? He's not just using a trick?" Penelope stared hard at her.

"Of course, I can't know that. But I can use my magic, and we need Raven's dreams." Kaia bit back with an annoyed huff. "We have been playing it safe for too long, Pen. Even if we get to the Chameleon Sprites, we have no idea how to fight Silas or what he's planning."

Penelope worried and bit her lip. "I know..."

Raven sighed as they stretched out, setting aside their mending. "It's the only plan we have. So, Kaia. Put me under."

Kaia glanced at Penelope, suddenly unsure of her plan. But Penelope nodded once, and Kaia placed her hands on Raven's head. She sucked in a deep breath, reaching for her magic.

"Sleep deeply," she said.

It was the only thing she could think of. But the magic tingled in her palms, running through her to Raven. Raven let out a sigh, and their whole body relaxed. It worked! Shaking slightly, Kaia kneeled back on her heels.

"Now, let's just hope we actually get something useful," Penelope murmured. "And that using magic doesn't tell Silas exactly where we are."

CHAPTER
TWENTY-FOUR

The storm blew over while Raven was sleeping. They were camping in a low area near a stream, with plenty of bushes to break the wind. They had stretched the canvases out into a makeshift lean-to, and it was surprisingly warm with the little fire they'd built in the space.

Penelope lowered the book she was reading. All the words seemed to run together, and she had difficulty absorbing any of them.

"This is worse than when I was studying for exams," Wickham groaned. He closed the book he was reading and rubbed his eyes. "Is Raven awake?"

They all looked at the bookbag. There was no movement from inside.

"We need to be patient," Herja advised. "These things aren't exactly an exact science."

Nolen and Finnegan were sleeping, so they kept their voices low. Kaia was still trying to read, a pucker between her brows. The dye that they had used on both her and Wickham was starting to fade, making their hair a patchy, muddy mess. Penelope couldn't help but think that her reflection would look ragged, too. She sighed.

"We should get moving again. Or at least get some more food."

Kaia's expression fell. "We really do, don't we? I don't like it, Pen. I feel like we're not getting anywhere. We need to have a better plan."

"Until Raven wakes up and tells us whether they could catch anything, it's our only plan," Penelope replied.

"The Sprites will at least be able to hide us from anyone who comes looking," Wickham offered.

Kaia shook her head, her expression darkening. "Unless Silas has something he can use against them, too."

Penelope flinched. It was the thing they didn't want to think about that they could put the Sprites in danger by going to the Golden Forest. She had a feeling that if Silas had something he could use against them, he'd already be using it, however. She didn't think it would make much difference—

The sound of a snapping twig made her jerk. Her head twisted, and her eyes skimmed the surrounding scrub brush. Movement caught her eye. A flash of purple—no woodland creature had that vibrant of color, least of all in winter.

She cried out as she jumped to her feet, snatching the long staff that Finnegan had carved her from a sapling.

Herja was also on her feet instantly while Nolen and Finnegan jerked awake. Kaia grabbed the pouch which held the mirrors and buckled it around her waist while Wickham crawled into the book bag.

A dozen armored warriors crashed through the trees. Finnegan lunged forward, wings snapping open from his shoulder blades. Penelope also planted herself before the others to give them time to get into the bag.

Something flashed through the air. A shiny dart pierced into Finnegan's chest, and he jolted, then dropped to one knee. His wings slowly retracted until they had disappeared altogether, leaving behind two jagged rips in his shirt.

The warriors surrounded them. They were on foot, and none of them had silver eyes. So, no dragons. But one of them was holding a long blow dart gun, and he loaded a fresh dart as he smiled at them.

"Rattleback venom," this man said. "It prevents a person from becoming a dragon, does it not?"

Penelope hissed through her teeth. She tightened her grip on her staff, but the warriors around them were armed with swords, maces, and other weapons. They didn't look like they would be so easily driven back as the guards in the town.

"I am your prince," Finnegan snarled as he pushed himself back to his feet. "You—"

"You are a traitor to the queen," the man with the blow-dart gun. He laughed, the sound of a low rumble. "At least, that's what we're saying, right? But she wants you back alive. Too bad she'll never know what happened to you. Even a dragon's body burns, doesn't it?"

A chill ran down Penelope's spine. "We're supposed to be brought back alive."

"On Rowena's orders," the man replied.

Finnegan drew his sword. "But not Silas's, is that right?"

Penelope's heart thudded. Did that mean that Rowena's deception hadn't worked? Did it mean that Silas was in charge and only used Rowena as a figurehead?

"If you resist... yes." The man lifted his blow-dart gun to his lips, aiming it at Penelope now.

She backed up a step, looking around wildly. They were pinned in with no way to run. Even if they could, they would have to leave behind their supplies. They'd freeze to death for sure! And if they tried to fight? Finnegan had a sword, sure. They had rough bows and arrows that were only good for killing small game.

They couldn't win this fight.

"What if we surrender?" she blurted.

Finnegan hissed again.

The warrior lowered his dart gun slightly. "He would prefer you alive, yes."

Was he telling the truth? Penelope closed her eyes, praying that he was. If only Raven were awake! She took a deep breath, dropped the staff, and held her hands out, ready to be shackled.

"Then we surrender," she said, not opening her eyes. "Finnegan, your sword."

A moment later, there was the clink of metal. Finnegan let out a ragged sigh. "Very well. We will surrender. They're only kids."

This was met by a snort and the rasp of metal rubbing against itself. Cold, hard manacles were latched over Penelope's wrists. Her hands dropped several inches. It was only now that she opened her eyes. Kaia, Nolen, and Finnegan were already shackled. The warriors locked the shackles over Herja's wrists.

"Where are the others?" the leader demanded. "The gorgon and the other boy?"

Penelope took a deep breath. Did she dare reveal their position?

Finnegan answered for her. "They're dead. Why do you think we're heading south? We separated in a storm, and when we found them, they were frozen. You want to see their bodies? Just follow the river north two kilometers."

The leader snorted again and turned on his heel, heading east. "Bring them," he said over his shoulder.

A warrior yanked on Penelope's shackles, nearly making her fall over. She grit her teeth and strode forward, keeping her head high.

From the corner of her eye, she saw Kaia tuck the strings of the book bag into her belt. Great big tears were falling down her face. The warrior seemed to be a bit more gentle with her... maybe they could use that to their advantage.

But how? Penelope had no idea.

Wickham pressed his ear to the opening of the book bag. He couldn't hear anything besides some muffled laughter. How long would this ruse work? How long before the warriors looked into the bag?

He slumped backward, resting his head against the wall. He and Raven were free... but what could he do about it?

As though in answer to his thoughts, Raven moaned. Wickham jumped, then scooted over closer to them. He pressed a hand over their mouth, preventing them from making more noise and alerting the warriors from finding the two of them.

"Shhh," he whispered, wishing to see if Raven was awake or asleep. "We've been taken prisoner."

Raven stirred, pulling their head away from Wickham's hand. They pushed themself into a sitting position and put a hand to their head. "How many?"

"I don't know." Wickham rubbed the back of his neck. "Did you see anything?"

"Not much," Raven admitted. "Just Silas standing at the seashore, holding back the rains. Then there were the gorgon mirrors, and I could see my own face in it, and as I looked at myself, the rain fell. Silas sat on a throne made of artifacts, but then the clouds burst, and a flood of rain washed him away."

Wickham's shoulders slumped. No, that wasn't much at all.

"We know Herja's theory is right, though," Raven said as they rubbed their neck. "Silas is hoarding artifacts, and that's how he can do all this. He's the one changing the weather patterns, too. I'm more certain now than I ever was before."

"It doesn't help our current situation, though," Wickham said helplessly. He gestured toward the entrance. "How do we get out of this now?"

Raven rolled to their knees. "I have an idea. But I need to get hold of those mirrors."

Kaia stumbled. Her feet were frozen. They hadn't given her the time to put her boots on, and she worried that if she looked back, she'd see her blood staining the immaculate snow. By this time, her false tears—the tears she'd used to get the guard to let her keep the bookbag—had dried up. Real ones had taken their place, though she fought against them.

"Did you say something?" the warrior asked suddenly, turning toward her.

Kaia blinked back at him. "Um, no?"

The warrior squinted at her, then glanced around. "Sure. You're muttering things and making me think I'm hearing ghosts."

Was he okay? Kaia stared incredulously at the man until she heard it, too. *"Listen."*

She hurriedly adjusted her gaze to stare straight ahead again, holding her breath. That was Wickham's voice! But she needed to get away from the warrior to talk to him without the warrior from hearing.

"I have to use the bathroom," she blurted.

The leader, the one with the dart gun, turned. Once they had emerged from the riverbed, he'd gotten onto a horse and put on a cloak of bear fur. He looked so cozy that Kaia was jealous.

"Do I look like I care?" he snapped.

Kaia's mind raced. The fake tears had worked at the town and against the warrior who shackled her, but she doubted they'd do anything with the leader. She let her lip tremble all the same as she lowered her gaze.

"I'm sorry, sir," she whispered. She took a deep breath and let tears slide down her face again.

"I'm sorry, sir," he repeated in a high, nasal voice, then laughed. "Do you think those tears are going to sway me? I've been assigned a mission, and I'll be rewarded by the Sorcerer when I deliver you."

She made herself stumble and fall to her knees, crying out as she did so. She hunched, pushing her face closer to the book bag. As she pressed her face into the snow, she realized the magic buzzed along her palms more strongly than ever. Silas might have found them because of the spell she used to put Raven to sleep—

Or these non-dragon warriors were already closing in on them when she did so.

She took another deep breath and pushed herself back to her feet, forcing herself to stumble as she could barely walk. As she did so, she reached out with her mind.

Wickham? She tried.

A jolt of surprise answered her, and then, *Kaia! Mind-to-mind is working again?*

I guess so—what do you need? She bit her lip as the warrior's leader narrowed his eyes, glaring at her as though he could imagine what was happening. She dropped her eyes and picked up her pace so the warrior beside her could no longer pull on her shackles.

The leader turned back, and Kaia sighed in relief.

I need the mirrors; Raven said mind-to-mind. They explained what needed to be done to Kaia, and she took another deep breath. Moving cautiously, she unbuckled her pouch and drew one of the hand mirrors. The warrior assigned to her was now looking straight ahead, a troubled look on his brow.

She loosened the mouth of the book bag and dropped the mirror in, then pulled the drawstrings from her belt and let it drop. The next part would be trickier. Her brow furrowed as she tried to think of how to do it.

"Sir," she called.

The leader turned again.

"I really do need to use the bathroom—perhaps my friends can circle me for privacy?" she held her breath.

"It can't hurt," the warrior with her said. "They surrendered easily enough."

The leader glared at him, then called a stop. The Odentia warriors lined next to the horse, drawing their weapons as they did so. Penelope, Herja, and Nolen moved in close to Kaia while Finnegan stayed closer to the warrior.

That wouldn't work.

"I need you to help make the privacy," she told him. Her voice was higher than usual, with a note of panic in it.

The Odentian warrior stirred on his horse, frowning.

Finnegan sidled closer, his expression twisted. Once he was close enough, Kaia plunged her hand into her pouch again. She drew the second mirror and jumped forward so her friends were behind her and the warrior's head. She held up the mirror, facing it back towards herself.

Bright light erupted from it, blinding her. Then a cold, swirling mist spun all around. It slipped into her lungs and clouded her eyes like she was turning to stone.

TWENTY-FIVE

N o. Not again.

Penelope's heart pounded in her throat. The glittering mist swirled all about her, so thick she couldn't see her hand when she waved it in front of her face. Panic welled up in her, but she didn't dare scream, terrified that the mist would pour down her throat and clog up her lungs, putting her to sleep like it had the last time.

Her eyes widened in the darkness, searching for anything besides these glimpses of flashing light that skittered across her vision. She could feel the mist seeping into her eye sockets.

A glow suddenly lit the darkness. The thudding of her heart slowed as a figure appeared in the middle of the light, a beacon for her to walk toward. Though she couldn't see the ground beneath her feet, she could feel it and headed toward the figure clothed in light.

As she got closer, a smile spread over her face. They were draped in fabric, wearing a dirty face veil and torn hood. Raven. The rest of Penelope's fears slipped away as she headed toward her mate. From the corners of her eyes, she saw piles of things. Swords, cloaks, boxes. At one point, there were shelves upon shelves of potions.

She reached Raven and felt the others next to her. She reached out wordlessly and caught a hand in hers. The mist faded a little around them.

"Everyone keep your eyes on me," Raven said as they backed away.

The panic crawled back up Penelope's throat. "Wait! Don't leave us!"

"I'm not leaving you, Pen," Raven replied. "Come with me."

Penelope took a deep breath, the taste of the mist metallic on her tongue. She pushed herself forward. A coldness gripped the back of her neck, and it felt like a deep mud was sucking her legs down, but she refused to stop. With her gaze locked on Raven, she pushed forward.

Two obsidian mirrors appeared through the darkness. They were huge, reaching so far upward that Penelope couldn't see their tops. The face of a giant appeared on one, eyes flashing with hatred. A roar echoed in her ears—Then Raven reached for her again, and she struggled forward, still clinging to her hand. She reached out with her free hand—

Blinding light.

And then she hit a hard wooden floor. The air was driven from her lungs, and even in the blinding white light, she thought she saw the mist expelled from her lungs.

Slowly, she became aware she wasn't the only one here.

Kaia choked on deep gasps for air beside her, and Wickham was trying to push himself upright and falling over every time. Herja lay on her back, staring up with wide eyes. Nolen was on his hands and knees, trembling. Finnegan lay with his face pressed into the cool wood.

"Stay still," Raven ordered. Penelope could hear them moving about. "Let your bodies recover."

The ceiling looked... familiar. Penelope blinked, her brow furrowing. After a few minutes, she placed it. They were in a cabin. Her head tilted, and she saw two bunk beds on either wall. Each bed had four drawers underneath.

"The Silent Marshes," she murmured.

She pushed herself to a sitting position, glancing out a window.

Sure enough, she could see the large, leafy trees that grew in the marshes beyond the glass.

"Yeah," Raven said as they knelt beside her. "We're at the marshes. As soon as we were inside the mirrors, I knew Silas knew we were there and would know where we went. I had to take us somewhere we could hide. I thought, there's lots of food in the marshes, and I can connect with the creatures that live here."

Penelope nodded. The motion made her stomach squeeze, but the weakness was passing. She pushed herself up, but something clanked and pulled on her wrists. Glancing down, she realized she was still shackled.

"Here," Wickham said, leaning over. The manacles he had been shackled with lay open on the floor. He ran his fingers over the cuffs, and they sprang over. "Since Silas already knows where we are, there's no point in hiding our magic."

Penelope nodded. She got to her feet and helped the others up as well. Finnegan seemed to struggle the most. But then, he was still dealing with the Rattleback venom in his system. His face looked green and clammy.

"We have to move fast," Raven said, putting both gorgon mirrors back into Kaia's pouch. "He has other mirrors. He'll be after us soon."

Penelope pulled Finnegan to his feet. "Let's get moving."

They headed out of the cabin. Kaia and Raven led the way this time, with Penelope and Finnegan taking up the rear. He still had to lean against her, his footsteps faltering.

"Why can't we use the bookbag again?" he groaned as they stepped into the forests.

"We don't have it," Herja said, her voice tense. "It was left behind."

Penelope swallowed. The bookbag is their only source of constant shelter. The only means they had of Finnegan carrying them every-where. The books. It was all gone. She tried hard not to let her spirit sink. They had the information they needed, right? And the weather was warm here. The Swamp was oddly dry, but the weather meant they wouldn't freeze to death... right?

They walked for some time, the silence of the marshes pressing in on them. Penelope shivered despite herself. She knew this space was silent for everyone other than witches, but it seemed ominous now. It was like they were back in their first year, never knowing when the villain would emerge from the trees to bring them down.

"I think I figured out how Silas uses the mirrors when he's not a gorgon," Herja said after some time. It appeared the silence was pressing too deeply on her, too.

"How?" Penelope asked, grateful for the conversation.

"While we were in that place, I saw other gorgon artifacts. At least they had the same patterns that the mirrors have on them," Herja said.

Raven nodded. "I saw them, too."

"I think he had a gorgon skull."

Raven stopped abruptly. They whirled, their hood sliding down on the hard coils of their snake-like hair. Quickly they covered it again and held the hood in one place. "What do you mean?" Their voice was bleak.

"There was a skull covered in these fine growths, like the gill bones of a fish," Herja replied. "I think he's using the skull to activate all the gorgon artifacts."

Penelope's stomach clenched. Horror clogged her throat. Disturbing the rest of the dead seemed unthinkable, especially for selfish gains. She supposed she shouldn't be so surprised... this was the man who was willing to kill them all, after all.

Herja took a deep breath. "If we can get the skull away from him, we will stop his powers. So that's what we have to do—"

"No." Finnegan straightened. His cheeks were still green, but he seemed stronger now. His silver eyes blazed with determination. "No, there will be no quests to steal the skull. We can't risk it. There's only one solution—we have to kill him."

***

The group hadn't stopped for rest until they found a brownie nest. There, Raven explained their situation to the brownies, and the brownies promised to spread through the Marsh and warn all the other nests, nymphs, kelpies, and other creatures they could find. A few of them hovered about, standing as watchers for the students in case Silas's men came at them.

They no longer had a pot to cook in, but Nolen found a hollow log to fill with water. By heating stones in a fire and dropping them into the log, they could heat the water to boiling and cook up a lovely dish of marsh weed-log soup. It was disgusting.

And delicious.

"You lived on this the whole time I was hunting you?" Finnegan asked him, poking at the long strands of weeds.

"We had no choice. We don't have much choice now, either. Eat. We're going to need our strength," Wickham said, picking out some of his own food. It was nothing to rave over, but it was hot and filling. "Come on, Finnegan. You were the one that found all those nuts to put into it."

Finnegan sat back, shaking his head. They were all gathered around the log, eating. "Sorry. I can't stomach it right now. Maybe later. You all get some sleep—I'll take first watch."

Wickham frowned. Finnegan had been relatively quiet all day, ever since they had all overruled him, and stated in no uncertain terms that they would not be a party to killing Silas. He said they didn't understand but left it at that.

He was right. They didn't understand. But then, he didn't either. This was just one of those situations where the discussion would not budge any of them. Wickham wasn't sure it was the right choice, letting Silas live.

But when he thought about taking a life? It made him too sick to his stomach to even think about it.

"Are you sure about first watch?" he asked, yawning. The hot food in his stomach was making him tired.

Finnegan stood and stretched his back. "I'm sure. The brownies can't do everything."

Wickham nodded. He laid out, pillowing his head in his arms. He'd stay awake a little longer, though, just in case—

He'd barely closed his eyes when they snapped back open. The fire had gone out entirely. A chill swept over him, and he staggered to his feet, his head feeling murky. The way it did when he was sick and took medicine that would help him sleep.

"Oh, no," he breathed.

The brownies buzzed around him anxiously. Night had fallen deeply around them. Quickly, he staggered to the log where their food was still in it. Leaning over it, he inhaled deeply. Under the scent of the marsh weed, there was a sickly-sweet odor reminiscent of roses and rotten fruit.

His stomach dropped. Eyeshade berries. A popular addition to any medications meant to put someone to sleep.

They'd been drugged. But how? Who—?

He looked around again as the others stirred. Everyone was here... except Finnegan and Raven. The nuts. Finnegan must have slipped in the berries when he added the nuts. He had been the one to drug them. But why?

Snarling, Wickham hurried to Herja's side. She groaned when he shook her, but her eyes opened, reflecting the moonlight.

"Wake up," he bellowed. "Finnegan's taken Raven somewhere. We have to follow them."

Herja closed her eyes and groaned again. She rolled over and covered her head with her arms. Kaia was stirring now. She crawled to Nolen, but no matter how she shook him, he would only roll over and fall back to sleep. Neither could Wickham wake Penelope.

"We have to leave them behind," Wickham said. His head still felt cloudy, the effects of the berries trying to pull him down. "Kaia, use your wand. We can follow where Finnegan took Raven."

Kaia nodded. She grabbed her pouch and reached inside, then gasped.

"What is it?" Wickham asked, his heart dropping. "Did he take your wand?"

"No."

"Then what?"

Kaia pulled out her wand and staggered to her feet. Her eyes were wide, and her skin paled in the moonlight. "The mirrors. He took the mirrors."

TWENTY-SIX

A bitter taste filled Kaia's mouth as she held her wand high, the light at the tip of it lighting their way. A half-dozen brownies buzzed anxiously ahead, leading them through the swamps. They seemed impatient for the two witches to move faster, but every time Kaia tried to go faster, she vomited.

"Finnegan overdosed us on those berries," Wickham growled as they pushed onward. "That's why we're like this. What was he thinking? He could have killed us!"

Kaia spat as another bit of last night's stew flowed into her mouth. She usually wasn't a fan of vomiting, but it was helping clear her head —maybe because she was getting the last of the berries out of her system.

She breathed deeply, bringing the cool air into her lungs. "It doesn't matter. He wouldn't have done this without a plan. We have to find them."

Why would he take Raven? His words from the previous day rattled around her skull. Was he trying to get Raven to send him to the Eldavon palace? Would he try to do that on his own? Why wouldn't he consider other options? Why not let them help him fight Silas, at the very least?

With a growl, she pushed herself harder. "We're going around in circles!"

One of their brownie guides swooped into her face, brandishing its tiny spear. It screeched at her, and she ducked, avoiding it.

"All right, all right," she said. "I'm sorry!"

Wickham groaned and stumbled off the path. The sounds of his retching in the bushes triggered her nausea, and the last of her dinner came up and out. Her head felt much more apparent, but her body was even weaker. Her legs shook as they continued.

They stumbled through thick shrubs, and the moonlight lit up the small clearing they entered. The brownies hung back, hiding among the foliage. The clearing was a flat plane, with dead, dried-out grasses lying flat against the ground.

Finnegan stood in the middle of the clearing. He held the mirror in both hands, glaring into the forest. The moonlight glinted off the mirror's obsidian face.

"Where's Raven?" Kaia demanded, looking around wildly.

Finnegan didn't so much as twitch to acknowledge her.

Her anger boiled over, her hand tightening on her wand. The light at the end flickered slightly as she strode forward. "Answer me! What are you planning? What have you done to Raven?"

"Kaia," Wickham called after her.

Kaia slowed. Finnegan still hadn't moved. He still held the mirror outstretched. His gaze remained fixed on a distant spot. His shirt billowed in the breeze but didn't respond to the cold. A fresh bitter taste crept up Kaia's throat. She lifted her wand higher, and the light glittered back off Finnegan's skin and hair.

She stumbled away, her jaw-dropping. She wanted to scream, but no sound came out. He had turned to stone. His hair, his skin, his eyes. He was a statue, staring straight ahead with a determined look, his hands outstretched with that mirror.

She couldn't hear past the blood rushing in her ears as Wickham approached her and grabbed her wrist. Kaia clung to him, her mind racing. Had he tried to force Raven to activate the mirror, and they'd had no choice but to take off their veil? Had he turned them over to Silas?

She wanted to ask, wanting something to break the silence. But a stone man could say nothing.

"Where's Raven?" she finally whispered, and her voice sounded like a boom in the silence.

Wickham dropped her arm. He turned on his heel to one side and headed for some bushes. Kaia watched him at first, then realized a whimpering in the direction he was heading. She steeled herself and headed that way, holding her wand high again so they could see.

"Raven?" she called.

Another whimper, this time accompanied by a rasping noise. Like... snakes. She hurried forward and grabbed Wickham's arm. He gave her a startled look, and she shook her head slightly, indicating to him to fall back.

"Raven," she said as she inched forward. The rasping grew louder. "Is that you?"

A sob answered her.

Kaia continued moving forward, ensuring the light was ahead of her so Raven could see her coming. She talked in a low voice, only getting louder as Raven's sobs grew louder. She stepped through the bushes to find Raven huddled on the ground, clutching their veil to their face while their hood lay on the ground. The snake-like coils of hair hissed and rasped against each other as they writhed.

"Kaia?" Wickham called.

"It's okay, we're here," Kaia called back. "But just stay there for now. I need to help them."

She knelt beside Raven, setting the wand down. The light snuffed out at once, but there was enough moonlight for her to continue to navigate. First, Kaia helped Raven to tie their face veil back into place. The ties had been ripped, so Kaia had to secure it with her own belt. Next, she pulled the hood over Raven's head.

The snake-like coils calmed as they were covered. The hard, glittering cases wrapped into a bun at the base of their neck. If Raven were in the water, those coils would open up to feather-like fans of gills.

Once Raven was covered once again, Kaia wrapped her arms around them. They buried their face into her shoulder and sobbed. Kaia rubbed their back, rocking them softly.

"What happened?" Kaia asked.

Raven shook their head and sobbed even louder. "I can't."

"It's okay," Kaia said. "You're okay now. Everything is going to be all right."

"I need Penelope," Raven whimpered. "I need my mate."

"I'll go get them," Wickham volunteered.

He disappeared, the brownies buzzing around him again to lead the way. Kaia held onto Raven, trying to comfort them. But the worry about what happened still ran in circles around her mind. What had happened?

<hr />

Penelope felt stronger than she had the previous evening when Finnegan drugged them. Her head was clear, and she felt like she could run the length of the swamp. Anger burned in her chest.

What had Finnegan been thinking? He'd drugged them all, and for what? To kidnap Raven? Her lips drew back into a snarl, and she almost didn't feel bad for him being turned into stone. What possible reason could he have for any of this? It didn't make sense!

Herja and Nolen followed her and Wickham, muttering to each other. Penelope blocked them out, not wanting to hear the theories about what Finnegan had been planning.

They got to the clearing quickly. By this time, the darkest part of the night had passed, and the glow of dawn lit the swamp. The first thing Penelope saw was the grey, cold statue of Finnegan. He stood in the center of the clearing, and as Penelope drew closer, she stared at his frozen face. Was that fear she saw intermingled with his determination?

They would never know now what he had been thinking.

She turned abruptly from the statue, her gaze skimming the tree line. Soon, she saw a sock hanging on a bush and rushed for it. She burst through the bushes to see Raven lying on the ground, their head on Kaia's knee. Their breathing was deep and even, and Kaia quickly put a finger to her lips.

"They just fell asleep," she whispered.

Penelope nodded as she sank to her knees. Relief tumbled through her so powerfully that she almost started crying. As much as Wickham had assured her that Raven was all right, she hadn't believed him until now. Her gaze moved down her mate's form. No sign of blood. That was good.

"Pen," Kaia breathed. She leaned forward to catch Penelope's face in her hands. The movement jostled Raven.

"Kaia," Penelope hissed. She was the one that had just told her to be quiet!

Raven lifted their head, then let out a cry and sprang forward. They wrapped their arms around Penelope and hugged her tightly. Penelope clung back to them, closing her eyes as she sent prayers of thanks to Sun, Moon, and Stars that they had made it out of this.

"Penelope, your eyes," Kaia cried. A smile slowly spread over her face.

"My eyes?"

Releasing a soft breath, Raven pulled back. Their hands lingered on Penelope's face as they gasped.

"They're silver again," Raven whispered.

Penelope touched her own cheek. She reached inside and felt the flicker of fire that she had been missing for far too long. A surprised laughter burst out as she straightened, bringing Raven to their feet.

The three of them entered the clearing. Kaia raced to Nolen, holding his face in her hands.

"We have our dragons back," Penelope announced.

Wickham gasped and hurried to Herja.

Penelope cast a look at the statue and shook her head. "We need to get to the palace right away."

She would have suggested reaching out mind-to-mind, but Raven was in no state to help with that. If this meant what she suspected that Silas was gone, then there was no need for urgency, either. Nothing that couldn't wait until Raven was calm enough to reach out, but for now, there was the urgency to get moving.

Her stomach growled, but she ignored it. They could find villages and towns to stop at for food on the way.

She took a deep breath and moved back a little, then closed her eyes. She was afraid for an instant that it wouldn't come easily and that she would have to relearn how to take her dragon form. But she felt her body stretch out, felt herself moving to occupy more space, and grinned.

She had never felt so free to be a dragon. She opened her eyes once more, finding herself towering over the clearing. Quickly, she lowered herself to the ground so Raven could climb onto her back, then leaped into the sky. Nolen, carrying Kaia, and Herja, bringing Wickham, were quick to follow. Penelope circled over the marshes once, trying to memorize the space where Finnegan was.

Then she was off through the clear blue sky. Her wings pumped hard as she sped toward the north, where the palace was. A calm wind blew after them, helping her go faster. She tucked her legs against her belly and lowered her head to streamline herself more.

Whatever Silas had done to them was reversed. That much was clear. But did it mean he was defeated? And if he was, how?

A possibility slipped into her mind, and she had to shove it away before she could shudder. No. She wouldn't think about that. For now, all she could concentrate on was getting to the palace. They would get their answers once they reached the Crown.

TWENTY-SEVEN

W hen they stopped at the first village, the people hid from them. It took several minutes before Penelope convinced them they were from Eldavon and needed food to take the necessary information to the palace. The people gave them some food but regarded them warily.

It was no wonder; it had been months since the dragons of Eldavon had lost their dragons.

"Maybe we can use the gorgon mirror to get us back to the palace faster," Kaia suggested as they ate. The sky was growing rapidly darker, and lightning flickered in the south.

"We can't," Raven said.

Penelope turned to them, her heart in her throat. It was the first thing they had said. "It's okay if you don't want to."

"No, we can't," Raven said. They sighed as they reached into the pouch and pulled out the mirror that was left. It had turned into a glittering grey stone. "They don't work anymore. I don't know what happened. But they're broken. They broke when Silas..."

They trailed off. Penelope moved closer and wrapped an arm around Raven's shoulders. "It's all right if you don't want to tell us," she intoned. "But maybe it will help us understand."

Raven shuddered, took a breath, and began talking.

Raven's head felt heavy as if someone shook them hard. They wanted to tell whomever it was to leave them alone that they were sleeping. Someone hissed into their ear, and it was so frustrating that they opened their eyes. They told whomever it was to do away, but then a hand pressed over their mouth.

The glow of a light stone irritated their eyes, and they blinked. Slowly, Finnegan's face came into focus. He held a light stone in his hand right in their face.

"The others are sleeping," he whispered. "But I need to talk to you. Come with me."

Raven repressed the urge to groan. They had seen how quickly Penelope and the others had fallen asleep. After being on the run for so long, the Silent Marsh finally gave them a place to be safe from Silas and his minions, at least for a little while. Raven didn't want to wake them.

They dragged themself to their feet, reaching under their veil to scrub their eyes. They were exhausted, too. What was so urgent that Finnegan couldn't wait until later to discuss it?

They yawned as they followed Finnegan away from the camp. Most likely, Finnegan would try to convince Raven to convince the others that violence was their only option. Raven had to admit they weren't sure what other options the group had, not when it was so clear that Silas wouldn't hesitate to use violence against them.

If they had lived their teenage lives in the general population rather than at the Institute, would they be quicker to violence? The Institute was heavily on finding ways to resolve conflicts without hurting others... probably because they were teaching dragons and witches that could quickly kill massive amounts of humans if they wanted to.

They finally came to the clearing, and Finnegan held up the gorgon mirror. Raven came to a stop, blinking in surprise.

"Why do you have this?" they demanded.

Finnegan grabbed their hand and thrust the mirror into it, then drew a knife and pressed it to their throat. Raven's breath hitched, and their eyes widened.

"What are you—"

"Activate the mirror," Finnegan snarled. His expression was murderous in the light stone's glow—no empathy in his eyes. "No arguing. Activate it now."

Raven opened their mouth and closed it again as the knife's point caught on their veil and dug deeper into their skin. They leaned back, trying to put more distance between them and the blade, but Finnegan grabbed a handful of their hood, preventing them from twisting away.

"Activate it."

They couldn't. No matter what plan he had, it couldn't be good. They couldn't do as he said; they had to resist. It was clear what he wanted. Using the mirror to escape the swamp and leave the rest of them behind. Raven ground their teeth together. No! No, they couldn't do this.

The knife pressed harder into their skin. They closed their eyes.

But what choice did they have? Raven took a deep breath as they activated the mirror. They held it up, angling it slightly away from themself. If Finnegan wanted to use it to escape, he wasn't taking them with him!

"Hold still," Finnegan demanded. He dropped the knife and light stone as he glared at the mirror. "Silas! I know you can hear me. You want these kids? Answer me."

Raven's heart plummeted. He was going to sell them out. And why wouldn't he? He wanted to keep his powers, and Silas was a powerful sorcerer. They had been foolish to trust him. Just like how he betrayed them on the Thunder Ridge!

Silas's face appeared in the mirror. A smirk passed over his face. "Ah, Prince Finnegan. How lovely to hear from you."

"Save the pleasantries," Finnegan snapped. "I'm talking to you to save my own skin here. Do you want these kids? I can get them to you. Especially the gorgon here."

He shook Raven roughly, twisting slightly away from them. He held the mirror in one hand, the other still on Raven's hood. His fingers squeezed around the coil of one of their gills, crushing the protective exoskeleton. Raven whimpered in pain.

"I could use the gorgon," Silas said slowly. "But where is this coming from? They would have been much more useful for me in Odentia, where I had them before you took them."

Finnegan barked out a bitter laugh. "A pang of false conscience. But I can give them to you now. All you have to do is open up this mirror. I've drugged the others; they won't put out a fight."

Raven cried out. Finnegan shook them again.

"Very well," Silas said slowly. "I'll open the mirror for you to come through and—"

Even as he was talking, Finnegan was on the move. He ripped the hood and veil off Raven in one swoop. As the cloth fluttered to the ground, he twirled the gorgon mirror in his hands, holding it in both, outstretched, toward Raven's face.

Silas cried out. His face in the mirror turned to surprise, then froze in place. Raven stumbled back, covering their face. As they collapsed to their knees, the only sound was their heartbeat in their throat. When they looked up, they knew what they'd see.

The smooth obsidian glass was brittle, the image of Silas's face etched in stone.

Finnegan hadn't moved. The light stone at his feet had snapped in half, from what Raven didn't know. The moonlight streamed all around them, but they knew.

They knew. And their head swirled. Their stomach rebelled. All they could do was collect their veil and hood. The others would be here soon. They'd find them. And at that moment, Raven didn't want to be found.

They knew what Penelope and the others would say once the six of them were back together. *It's not your fault.*

And maybe it wasn't. But two men were turned to stone now, and all Raven could do was clutch the veil to their face and sob, fighting against sleep... because if they fell asleep with their face uncovered? Who else might see them?

Kaia's heart constricted as they blew into the palace on the edge of a storm. They had been delayed several days because of the rains, which were so thunderous that Kaia was now afraid of the topsoil erosion it would cause. But they had rain.

Reaching out to the Crown hadn't worked. But they were here now.

The three dragons swooped low into the central courtyard. Dozens of people were in the courtyard already, dancing in the rain. Whoops rose to greet them as Nolen came to a soft landing. Kaia slid down his slippery back, her legs and arms aching from clinging to him so tightly.

"Nolen!" Odele cried. She raced through the crowd to tackle her brother.

Other classmates emerged in the crowd. Kaia laughed and hugged them, asking again and again if they were all right. Rhett, Wickham's brother, leaped onto him and cried. Penelope kept her arm tightly around Raven as their classmates ran to her.

She caught Kaia's eye, and Kaia sobered. Right. They were here for a reason.

"We need to talk to the Crown," she announced loudly. "I'm sorry, we must get inside and see them."

Adina's smile faltered, but she nodded. "They're all in the central rooms. You might not be allowed to see them, though."

"We'll take that chance," Penelope said grimly.

The six of them moved through the crowd, which seemed reluctant to part for them. Kaia's heart pounded as they hurried inside. Had Silas done more damage than they knew? Had anyone died? It made tears burn against her eyes to think about it, but she tried not to dwell.

There was only one way to find out, and they were already headed on their way to do that.

The six of them came to the central rooms. To Kaia's relief, Kiango, Saffron, and Professor Farrow guarded the door.

"Row!" Herja squealed, racing forward. She hugged her adoptive parent tightly, and Row hugged her just as tightly. "I was so worried."

"You were worried?" Row demanded, their voice thick.

Herja released them and stepped back. "We need to speak to the kings and queens. It's essential regarding Queen Rowena of Odentia."

Row nodded. They reached for the door, and Kiango made a strangled noise.

"They are not to be disturbed," he said.

Row sighed. "These six will be their exception."

Kiango hesitated, then chuckled softly as he moved aside. "You know what? I think you're right."

Kaia nodded her thanks at him as they passed through. The two kings and two queens sat around the table in the circular room they entered. Lantos, Johanna, Sydney, and Abigail. Sydney had his arm in a sling, and Johanna sported a nasty-looking bruise on her cheek, but they otherwise seemed unharmed.

The four who made up the Crown stared in shock as the six students entered.

"You're alive," King Sydney said as he got to his feet. "You're... you're really alive!"

"We are," Kaia agreed. She gave him a tired smile. "And so are you. All of you. Did anyone...?"

Queen Johanna's face fell into anguish. "Three palace guards did not make it out of Rowena's attempted takeover alive."

Kaia winced.

"I'm so sorry," Penelope said, lowering her head.

"They died for their kingdom," King Lantos replied.

Kaia closed her eyes. Grief welled in her. Three lives were lost to Silas. It seemed far too high. She knew it could have been much worse, but just because it could have been worse didn't mean those three loyal guards didn't deserve to be mourned.

"And Silas?" Nolen asked.

"Turned to stone. No doubt thanks to—"

"Finnegan," Raven interrupted. "Prince Finnegan of Odentia sacrificed himself so we could defeat Silas."

Kaia took a deep breath, setting aside her grief for the moment. She would allow herself to feel it later. "And speaking of, where's Rowena? I know what it looked like and how she came to take over, but that's not true. She was the one who got us out of Silas's clutches in the first place. She made sure we could go free to defeat him."

The kings and queens glanced at each other, looking doubtful.

King Lantos went to the door and opened it. "Bring us six more chairs," he ordered. "We'll be here for a while."

Saffron answered in the affirmative; then King Lantos shut the door.

He turned back to the six students and folded his arms. "Now. Let's start at the beginning. What happened?"

CHAPTER
TWENTY-EIGHT

"I see," Queen Abigail said as the six finally finished explaining everything that had happened on their journey.

Herja nodded as she leaned back, folding her hands over her stomach. When the six of them revealed how they hadn't taken much food on the journey here—so as not to take too much from the villages they stopped at—the kings and queens had food and drink brought. Herja had never been much for apple juice, but she finished it with delight.

Lantos and Johanna were leaning against one another; by this time, Sydney had had to lie down, so a sofa had been brought into the room. One of Silas's potions had severely injured him, though it left no physical mark. Abigail sat on the sofa with him, combing her fingers through his hair.

It was odd that Herja felt so at ease with them, so comfortable not using their titles anymore. She had spent so much time with them, especially after Row adopted her, that she certainly saw them as people rather than an elusive crown.

Kaia leaned against the table. "So, you see, Rowena was playing the part she needed to keep Silas from turning on her, too. She was the one that made sure that bounty hunters would not kill us."

"I'll have her brought here," Lantos said as he stood. "What she's told us since Silas's defeat has corroborated with what the six of you have said. But you must understand this might not be the end of it. Regardless of whether she was playing a role, she attempted a takeover of Eldavon."

Herja nodded. It would take time to reassure the people of Rowena's true intentions.

"Hector will be pleased," Sydney said. "He's been here for some time, begging us to release her."

Kaia straightened, her eyes brightening. "He's okay, then?"

"Yes."

Lantos went to the door and murmured to the dragons posted outside it. Shortly after, Rowena was brought in. She looked exhausted, with dark smudges under her red, puffy eyes. When she saw the students, though, she brightened.

"You're all okay," she said, a grin on her face. Her expression faltered as she looked around. "Where's my uncle?"

Herja flinched. She glanced at the others, not wanting to be the one to say it out loud.

There was a scrape of chair legs against the stone floor as Kaia stood. She hurried over to Rowena and hugged her as she described, in short detail, what had happened. Finnegan had set a trap for Silas and ensured he could no longer harm her.

Tears welled in Rowena's eyes as she nodded, releasing Kaia. "Thank you. I wish I could have said goodbye."

Lantos cleared his throat. "We have made some progress using the Silver Springs regarding the beings trapped in gorgon stone. It may work for you tospeak with him again. In any case, we will work to restore him."

At this, Penelope put her arm around Raven. Raven leaned tiredly into her side, letting out a soft sigh.

Rowena gave the kings and queens an uncertain look. She clasped her hands before herself as she took a deep breath. "You have all been very kind to me. Kinder than I could have expected, considering my actions. Is there anything I can do to prove that I am telling you the truth?"

"There may be," Johanna said. "For now, we will cautiously accept your order of events thanks to these six corroborating."

"Thank you." Rowena bent her head, her shoulders slumping with relief.

Abigail cleared her throat, still on the sofa with Sydney, though he was sitting up. "Since we have established this, I think it's best if the young people are given rooms to rest now. It's been some time, as I understand, that they have been able to be comfortable.

"As much as I'm sure we would all love that, there's more we have to discuss," Raven sighed. They straightened and clasped their hand over the table. "I don't think Queen Rowena needs to be here for the discussion."

"Do I?" Kaia asked, her brow furrowed.

Raven cocked their head to one side. "I suppose not really. It will be all right if you want to go with the queen. This concerns what Penelope and I learned on our quest over the last year."

Ah, magic being unbalanced. Herja considered her place in all this as Nolen and Wickham excused themselves—but not before Wickham insisted on giving Sydney a magical perk up. Penelope insisted she wished to stay with Raven, and Herja rested her hands on the table.

"I have things to add to this discussion as well."

The kings and queens nodded their assent to her staying.

Once the others had left, Raven took a deep breath. It was clear they were exhausted but pushing past it to explain everything.

"Silas may have used artifacts to cause the drought over our and the other kingdoms," Raven said, leaning against the table. "But he wasn't entirely wrong about magic being unbalanced. Yes, he took advantage of it and made it worse, but it started before him."

Herja frowned. She hadn't heard this theory before.

"How do you mean?" Lantos asked gently.

"In the old stories, magic was everywhere, not just in Eldavon. And yet we've been centuries, millennia even, with magic staying within our unchanging borders. Why do you think this is? We know that there are more springs than the Silver Springs... were the others stopped up? Were they hidden?"

Johanna's brow puckered. "I don't understand how this brings magic into being unbalanced."

Raven nodded slowly. "I know. It's difficult for me to express what my thoughts are... but what are the people outside our borders? They aren't dragons or witches. Are they human? We were always taught that the Earth's magic reveals humans in a being. Can they have their magic if they don't drink from the springs?"

Shock crossed the king and queen's faces. Herja bit her lip—she had never thought of it that way before. But it made sense.

"Humans are meant to be the balancing force in our world. We've been so caught up with how other kingdoms will use the powers of dragons and witches that we've forgotten about humans," Raven continued softly. "And I don't know what we are meant to do about it. Unless we fix the unbalanced magic, more people like Silas will keep coming."

Herja cleared her throat, a sudden excitement coursing through her as she straightened. "I have something to say, too. It's not directly related, but it loops back to this. I hadn't considered it before, but I made a connection."

"Go ahead," Abigail said.

Herja took a moment to gather her thoughts, then spoke, "We know that there are other beings in Eldavon that can create rains like the rocs. And we know Raven can communicate directly with them. We also know that the winds from the sea bring rains throughout the kingdom, and the weather patterns disturbed, causing the drought."

"Yes," Lantos said slowly like he was trying to figure out where she was going with this.

"I propose we start seriously studying the connections between everything: mountains, seas, land, all of it. And figure out if and how we can nudge weather patterns so we don't have to face this sort of thing again," Herja explained.

She took a moment to gauge the reaction to her words to continue. "We can work with the rocs, mermaids, krakens, kelpies' all the previously ignored beings because we didn't know how to communicate with them. This will help us understand and give us more options to work as a united front for all our interests."

"That puts a lot of pressure on Raven," Penelope said.

Raven nodded. "But I will do it."

"And... maybe we also need more gorgons. One point has more difficulty balancing something than two, three, or more..." Herja trailed off, squinting at Raven.

They didn't seem more tense at this prospect, but they also pulled their hands into their lap, hiding them from view. Penelope narrowed her eyes, but not into a glare. Instead, she looked like she was struggling with her own initial reaction to Herja's words.

"I'm not sure that would be wise," Lantos said slowly.

"If the volunteers know what they're getting themselves into, it won't be as great a shock," Herja explained.

Raven cleared their throat. "She may have a point. But before we even consider this, I should go back to the Thunder Springs and see if I can connect to the ancient gorgons again. Oh, and I should talk with Tidebreaker. Such an ancient Kraken will know more about these things than I do."

"Ancient gorgons?" Johanna repeated.

"It's a long story," Penelope replied.

Johanna nodded, rubbing her forehead. "Regardless, let's return to Herja's proposal about controlling our weather patterns. I'm not sure it's good to mess with nature, but even if possible, it will take massive amounts of magic. Perhaps all the witches in the kingdom."

"Witches and dragons," Herja corrected. She took a deep breath, steeling herself. "And this is where it loops back to what Raven was saying about unbalanced magic. We'd have to open the Silver Springs to other kingdoms because we don't have enough witches and dragons in Eldavon for this."

The kings and queens looked distinctly unsettled by this. They glanced at one another, and Herja could see the resistance in their eyes. She clasped her hands a little tighter.

"I know it goes against so much of what we have done traditionally. But we are changing as a society; we've said it before. And sometimes, change is uncomfortable. Would our neighbors be so eager to invade if they had their own magic?"

"Would they resist invading if they had dragons of their own?" Lantos asked.

Herja shook her head, not knowing how to answer that. "Which is why I'm not the one who makes this decision... and I have to wonder if it's a choice for our kings and queens to make on their own. Or if perhaps there needs to be a vote on the matter. I don't know."

"But magic is unbalanced," Raven repeated softly. "And we must find a way to bring it back into balance. The only question is... how?"

TWENTY-NINE

K aia stood at the entrance to the small stone building in which the Silver Springs was housed. She smiled as Rowena exited the cabin where the children would come out in a few months. This year, she and Nolen had volunteered to be part of the greeting committee for the children who had turned thirteen.

First, though, Rowena had undergone the same journey. Kaia, Nolen, Penelope, Raven, Herja, and Wickham walked with her. They would return to the Institute for their final exams soon, but in the meantime, they had told Rowena all the stories about the first dragons, witches, and humans. She had eagerly drunk it all up.

"I suppose this is it," Rowena said. She bit her lip as she peered through the doorway of the building. "And Hector's waiting for me on the other side?"

"Yes," Kaia assured her.

Rowena nodded as she came forward, twisting her hands together. She looked as nervous as Kaia had felt all those years ago.

The discussion of whether to open the Silver Springs to other kingdoms was still under vote, but Rowena had been invited to drink; officially, it was thanks for her role in protecting Eldavon and because she was married to a dragon. Unofficially, it was to help reassure the people of Eldavon that other kingdoms weren't so different from themselves.

One of the major things halting the vote from moving forward was a new suggestion that other kingdoms are not allowed to drink unless they showed a certain amount of improvement to their social infrastructure, the sort of work Rowena was currently introducing into Odentia. Kaia wasn't sure exactly where she fell in on all of this, but she planned to seriously study all the sides before it came to a vote.

"Well." Rowena cleared her throat. "Shall we?"

Kaia opened the door and stepped in. The stone building was warmer than outside, thanks to the small fire on one side of the springs. Sunlight streamed through the windows, glinting off the clear waters that rippled into a pool and drained away through underground channels.

"It's beautiful," Rowena said as she stepped in. She lifted her face to the sunlight, then looked to the mirror at the end of the room. "That's not a portal mirror, is it?"

"No," Kaia assured her. "Just a regular one."

Rowena nodded. She stepped forward again, squaring her shoulders.

"It's all right, and it won't hurt," Kaia told her.

"Not even if I'm unworthy of magic?"

"The Silver Springs doesn't punish people," Kaia replied. She took the cup from its place and handed it to Rowena. "When Finnegan drank from it, it revealed him as human. And I like to think that it did help him, even though he was disappointed."

Rowena's head bowed slightly as she took the cup. "I think it did, too. When we returned to Odentia afterward, he seemed more centered. More at ease in himself."

Kaia stepped back, folding her hands behind her back. Rowena turned the cup in her hand, then knelt. She scooped up some water and closed her eyes as she sipped at it.

She stood ahead once she had finished the whole cup, her eyes still shut. Kaia examined her. Rowena's hair was still dark, and there was no noticeable change to her. She took the cup and put it back, and when she turned, Rowena was still frozen in the spot, breathing rapidly while her eyes were shut.

"Let's look," Kaia offered, taking her hand. She led Rowena to the mirror and positioned her in front of it.

Rowena slowly opened her eyes. They were dark, the same as they were before. They darted over her reflected image, taking in her face, her hair, everything. Eventually, she released a deep breath.

"Human," Kaia told her.

Rowena touched her own face. "I feel different, though."

"Oh? Different how?"

Kaia hadn't ever talked to the human adults she knew about what they felt when they drank from the springs before.

Rowena studied herself for a long moment before she turned to Kaia. "I feel... more confident. Stronger, somehow. I don't know how to explain it. But I know that I'm different, and I'm never going to be the same."

"And that's what it means to drink from the Silver Springs."

Kaia opened the door leading outside. Hector was waiting, pacing, but he stopped when he saw Kaia exit. His silver eyes glowed with excitement, his eyes remaining on the door. Rowena stepped out, and on seeing him, she blushed.

"Well?" She spun in a circle. "How do I look?"

Hector beamed at her. "Beautiful."

He rushed over to her, caught her in his arms, and kissed her. Rowena threw her arms around his neck, and Kaia looked away to give them privacy. "I'll go get lunch ready," she said.

"Thank you," Hector said. "We'll be eating in the bathhouse over there," he added, pointing. "I have a surprise for Rowena."

Kaia nodded once and left them alone. As a married couple, they would have a lot to talk about. She headed for the kitchen, where Nolen was already at work. She fell quickly into step beside him, seeing what needed to be done at a glance and joining in.

"Well?" Nolen asked.

"Human."

"Is she disappointed?"

"No. She seemed... happy," Kaia replied. She considered a moment, then sighed. "I'm still not sure where I stand on all of this, but I think Raven has a point about the balance of magic needing to be outside Eldavon, too. At least the other kingdoms accept the proposals to exchange labor in Eldavon for food."

"At least there's that," Nolen agreed.

The fear of war wasn't entirely over but hope for the future was brighter. With the statue of Silas locked away and the artifacts being retrieved from the space between the gorgon mirrors, Eldavon still had much work ahead of itself.

But it was good work, Kaia thought. And they had the chance to make their future even brighter than it had ever been before.

She grinned at Nolen, a sense of peace settling over her. "It's all going to work out, isn't it?"

Nolen grinned back at her. "I think so."

"Yeah. It's going to work out."

⁂

Penelope and Herja opened the windows under the bathhouse, letting the steam and heat escape. A fire blazed against a concrete base through which copper pipes had water flowing through them. The fire heated the water, allowing the bather to lounge in warm water.

"You think we can go up and see?" Herja whispered to her. "Or would that be wrong?"

Penelope considered, then shook her head. "We should give them privacy. It's been months since Rowena saw him, after all."

Herja nodded. The two slipped out from beneath the bathhouse; the fire was nicely contained but would continue to smolder for some time. The tub above was big enough for Rowena and Hector to talk with Finnegan.

"I guess it's better he should live here in the springs than remain a statue forever," Penelope mentioned as they headed for the cabin, which held the wood supply for the rest of the buildings.

She couldn't imagine what it was like, to exist like he was. He was fully conscious while he was frozen in stone. It made her shudder and made her feel sorry for Silas, too. It was a terrible prison to be trapped in. The Crown was still debating just what to do about him.

Finnegan, however, was permitted to live here at the summit of Mount Eldavon. He had to be always drenched in the spring water to remain free from stone, but he seemed to take it well. Not that Penelope talked to him often.

She and Herja entered the bunkhouse where the six of them were staying. Wickham and Raven were already there, weaving wreaths out of evergreens. It was a new idea Wickham had come up with to create crowns of living plants and imbue them with healing properties for chronic conditions.

Penelope slid into the seat next to him, sighing. "So, we'll be heading back to the Institute soon."

"For the last time as students," Raven said. "I wish I could have been there longer. It's been... pretty incredible."

"With any luck, once we've graduated, we won't have to keep saving the world," Herja cracked. "That will be for the next generation of kids."

Penelope laughed at that. Yes, it had been an incredible coincidence that they had ended up in all the situations they had... or perhaps not. They learned a great deal about themselves and the world through their adventures. Maybe the Sun, Moon, Stars, and Earth had all conspired to use them to create the change the land needed.

Kaia and Nolen slipped in, bringing with them a platter of sandwiches. They took the two empty chairs and settled down, grinning at each other as they ate.

"I'm going to miss seeing you all every day," Penelope said, a lump rising in her throat. "I love you all."

Herja bumped her shoulder. "Love you, too, Pen. And I'll miss you all too. But it's going to be a good thing. We'll keep in touch, and if any of you ever need me, I'll be there."

"Same," Wickham agreed. "In a heartbeat."

The others all nodded.

"I'll be writing you all often," Kaia said. "Although I don't expect you to write to me as often as I write to you... I've already gotten started on the emotional notes."

She laughed. Penelope shook her head, chuckling. Writing letters to each other was good. It would allow them to stay connected, at least. They had all been through so much together. It felt weird to plan on going their separate ways.

Penelope still knew it was for the best. They all had too much learning and growing to do yet. Their journeys were far from being over. But even if their paths would take them in different directions, it would always lead them back together. They had been bonded together in the face of a great adversary, and even though they might never have the Institute to bring them together again, that didn't mean they would be truly parted.

And besides letters, she said, speaking mind-to-mind to all of them. *We can close our eyes and still be together as long as we have our thoughts.*

So poetic, Raven teased back.

True, though, Nolen answered.

Kaia nodded. *Together always, as long as we want to be.*

Wickham and Herja grabbed each sandwich and held them up into the air like they were lifting glasses for a toast. *Hear, hear!*

Penelope grinned, eager to see what the next leg of their lives would bring. Trials? Sure. Happiness? For certain. Whatever came next, she was ready. They all were. And it would be glorious.

EPILOGUE

Three Months Later

Penelope grinned as she stepped into the dorm with the rest of the fifth-year dragons following behind them. They were all dripping wet, having had to perform their final physical exam in the rain. The course had been slippery, but they had all passed with time to spare.

"You did amazing," Odele gushed to Herja. "When you jumped from the last bar, I thought you would hit your head, but you pulled it off magnificently."

Herja laughed, shaking out her black hair. "Oh, I had to jump. I would have lost my nerve being that high if I hadn't! I think that last course was more about showing us what we can do than the teachers."

"Agreed," Odele said with a nod.

The witches were sitting near the fire, and several of them disappeared into the bedrooms, then returned with towels which they handed out to the dragons.

"This year was pretty incredible," Odele said, toweling off her blonde hair. "Even though I never want to go through that again, I learned something about myself because of that Silas's work. I put too much of my identity into being a dragon."

"Me, too," Xena agreed.

Penelope wrapped her own hair and stripped off her outer shirt to squeeze out over the fire. "So what are you going to do, then?"

Xena hummed as he dried off his arms. "I'm not sure. I'm considering culinary school."

"I'm getting a job in janitorial services while Adina goes through school," Odele replied. "I want to build up my general skills. I don't know how to clean a house."

Penelope chuckled. They would soon have their official graduation from the Institute, and then the world was opened for them to explore what they would do. She was still joining the military, but rather than preparing for war, she would learn how to better act in Eldavon's best interests. At the same time, she and Raven worked with the various other beings in Eldavon and beyond.

Already, Raven had successfully brokered an agreement with the rocs for them to bring storms and rains over crop fields that needed it in exchange for food. The rocs were temperamental and hard to convince but had finally agreed.

The Crown was still debating whether it was wise to try to purposefully create new gorgons. So far, Raven had had little luck contacting the ancient gorgons in the Thunder Springs, but they would not give up.

As though sensing her thoughts, Raven lifted their head. Even hidden as their face was, Penelope could feel their grin. Their spell book rested on their knee, the emerald-green cover glittering in the firelight. It didn't record spells like for the witches, but rather the knowledge Raven rained about their powers and recorded down all of their dreams.

So far, it seemed to Penelope that this spell book would also soon record prophecies. And then it would be far easier for Raven to see what needed to be done for all of them.

I love you, Raven told her.

Penelope smiled back. *I love you, too.*

Two Days Later

Wickham lifted his face to the warm spring sun. His fingers were twined through Herja's as they walked along the path to the pond, past the swinging bench where they had spent so much time, with Herja reading her novel to him. It all seemed too close, and yet so far.

"Now that exams are done, I wish we could stay a little longer," he said, shrugging once.

Herja laughed. "I know what you mean. This place has come to feel like home, hasn't it?"

"Yeah. And I know Rhett doesn't need me, but I want to stay for him. I want to return to my family to look after Donnelly and Tara." Wickham chuckled to himself as he shook his head in amusement. "I always thought that when I graduated, I'd suddenly be ready to go out and never look back."

"Looking back is a good thing, however. Remembering where we came from." Herja squeezed his hand. "Just so long as we don't get lost in the past."

Wickham nodded. They fell silent as they headed up the hill to the swinging bench. He was enrolled full-time in medical school and only had a few weeks to get moved into his new apartment before classes started. It seemed like it was happening so fast, even though he'd had lots of time to get used to it all.

"And I still intend to be queen one day," Herja said as they sat and swung. "That's going to take much work. But you were right when you told me to make it an end goal rather than what I'm working for as soon as I graduate."

Wickham nodded his agreement. They would be working together in the field once they both graduated. Herja wanted to work in the education sector, but it heavily overlapped with the medical center. She wanted to see if the medical techniques that doctors were taught could help with the mind to improve accommodations for kids and adults, both of whom were currently slipping through the cracks.

"Oh, did Kaia tell you?" Wickham asked, suddenly reminded of the news. "Rowena and Hector are expecting their first child together. I expect we'll be receiving invitations to the celebrations soon."

"Yeah. That's exciting," Herja said as she leaned into his side. "And them having a baby will certainly help give them a better position to implement all their plans for social change."

"They do have a fight ahead of them, don't they?" Wickham murmured. "There will always be a push and pull when it comes to change working against the comfort of what is."

"Yeah," Herja agreed. She pushed a little harder so they swung higher. "Change can be terrifying, just like how it's a big change for us to graduate like this. But I'm glad I've learned how to adapt to change. Even if it's not easy sometimes."

Wickham chuckled and kissed the top of her head. "I'm glad I learned how to change, too."

They sat there, gazing over the Institute grounds, and a pang hit Wickham's stomach. There was a great deal of change coming. Some of it exciting, some of it scary. But all of it good. He held Herja closer.

"I love you," she said.

"I love you, too."

<hr />

Three Days Later

Kaia hugged Penelope and Raven tightly before Penelope shifted to her turquoise dragon form. Raven climbed onto her back, and Kaia retreated, biting her lip to stop herself from crying as the two took off. Raven wore a dark grey travel suit, and with their hood and veil fluttering in the wind, they looked very regal and imposing as Penelope gained altitude and took off.

"And they're off to start their new adventure," Kaia said, making herself grin. Even though it was painful to say goodbye for now, she was thrilled about the growth her friends would be undertaking.

She then turned to Herja and Wickham, hugging them each in turn. "I'm rooting for both of you."

Herja squeezed her back as Wickham hugged Nolen goodbye. "We're both rooting for the two of you, too. I expect lots and lots of details about everything you see overseas."

Kaia's lip trembled.

She was looking forward to this so much. She would be working closely with King Sydney as he traveled over the seas to negotiate trade agreements and bring the offer to kingdoms there to drink from the Silver Springs. Nolen would accompany them, of course, and learn how to work on the ships as he always wanted to.

But there was also something about this that made it so clear how officially over her childhood was. They were graduates from the Institute, taking on official, meaningful work for the kingdom. It was terrific and nerve-wracking all at the same time.

"Take care of yourselves," she said as she stepped back.

Wickham grinned at her. "You take care of yourself, too."

Herja slipped into her ombre purple-blue-emerald dragon, and soon they were off, too.

Kaia wiped the tears that dropped down her cheeks, laughing at herself.

"It's okay to be sad. This is an ending of sorts," Nolen told her. He wiped a tear from her cheek.

"I know." She wrapped her arms around his neck and laughed as she kissed him. "But it's a beginning, too. I'm just feeling a little guilty about not telling anyone that we secretly had our official binding in secret."

Nolen's expression grew troubled. "Did you change your mind? Do you want to tell everyone?"

Kaia shook her head. So much of her life was shared with people, and she knew that her life would continue to be shared just as much. It felt right to have this just be the two of them for now. It seemed to be more about them, somehow.

"We'll share when the time is right," she said.

Nolen grinned at her. "Just give the word."

"You can give the word, too," she reminded him.

"Oh, I know." He laughed and kissed her again.

Kaia let her eyes shut. Yes, their friends were all going their separate ways, but she was looking forward to when they could gather again and again, sharing everything happening in their lives. This was a good thing.

"I love you," she whispered into Nolen's lips.

Nolen grinned. "And I love you, too. Forever and ever and ever."

"Don't forget for all eternity," Kaia joked.

"Eternity," Nolen replied. "Endlessly."

One Week Later

Herja released a shaky breath as she turned in a circle, viewing her relatively sparse apartment. It was the first time she would live on her own. As much as she had convinced herself she was a loner as a child, she had never been really alone. And now she was going to be entirely responsible for herself.

Well. Mostly.

Row and Wickham carried in the sofa, the last piece of furniture she now owned. It was Row's old sofa, but they had gotten a new one, so Herja inherited this one, which was good.

She and Wickham would live across the hallway from each other. All it would take was two steps out the door to get to his place. But while Herja had a single-bedroom apartment with a living room, Wickham had elected a studio-style apartment. His housing was provided for by the medical school he would attend, but he figured he needed little space, and the larger apartments could go to people who needed them more.

Part of Herja wanted to suggest they just live together, but that seemed like too much for them right now. No, it was best that they learned how to maintain their homes first rather than trying to figure it out together.

"Where do you want it?" Row asked.

Herja snapped back to the sofa. "Right, there is fine. I still don't know how to arrange everything, but I'll move it when I'm ready."

Row and Wickham set the sofa down.

"Feeling overwhelmed?" Row asked, smiling at her.

Herja nodded. "Yeah. But it's good."

"I know how you can feel unbalanced when you first move out on your own. You can contact me at any time," Row assured her.

Herja smiled back. It was less the moving out that made her feel unbalanced and more that she wasn't entirely sure what to do with herself. She had abruptly taken a gap year before returning to school. She was too comfortable in the classroom and needed to challenge herself.

Her mind would not be idle, however. She'd had a few ideas of how to reverse the effects of Raven turning Finnegan into stone permanently. He couldn't live in the water forever; he had to dry off and become stone again whenever he got too wrinkled. In any case, there had to be a way to fix the issue.

"Well. Your cupboards are full, and all your furniture is moved in," Row said. They grinned at her, but moisture glistened in their eyes. "I guess it's time I let you settle in."

Herja bit back on the sudden burning sensation in her eyes. "It hardly feels fair that I'm already moving out when we have had little time actually to live together as a family is a lot more than proximity." Row hugged her. "You will always have a home, Herja."

Herja hugged them back tightly. Then it was time to say goodbye, and they left.

Wickham smiled at her. "It's exciting, isn't it? Even if I want to cry right now."

"It is. Because this is the start of our life together." She put her arms around his neck and kissed him. "I love you."

"I love you, too."

Herja kissed him once more, then stepped back, rolling up her sleeves. Time to get to work! There was a lot left to do.

The End

If you enjoyed this book, please consider leaving a review on
Goodreads, Bookbub or your favorite retailer.
Reviews help me reach new readers.

Stay tuned for a <u>bonus novella</u> coming in the fall of 2024! Join my newsletter so you don't miss out!

Have you read **The Evers Series** and the **Blood Magick Trilogy**?

www.mhlebeault.com